RAT

Priscilla B. Shuler

Prelude

T he *Cross and Fly Pub and Inn* was well established just a few streets up from the London docks and the many storage warehouses. At the turn of the century, ushering in the 1800s, as the docks were being planned, enlarged, and established, so too the attendant outshoot inns and feeding stations were expanding. It was here that Eddie Cavendish helped in the construction of the sturdy building for which his uncle Boris had provided the funds. Boris was Eddie's mother's eldest brother and had inherited a fairly decent fortune from their father. Being as how Uncle Boris never was able to produce a legitimate heir, Edward Cavendish became the favored one to become the proud owner of the lucrative business upon the death of Uncle Boris.

Abigail Worthington was the beautiful red-haired daughter of the family Boris had hired to run the establishment. Without much ado, Abigail and Eddie were soon wed, upon which Edward was immediately installed as the sole owner of *The Cross and Fly*. The place proved to be especially sought out by the influx of foreign sailors and travelers. The food was excellent and the rooms were clean. Eddie and Abigail ran an enviable business.

London, during this time of development, had very little in the way of sewage disposal. Mostly what was thrown out flowed downhill over the cobblestones. Thus, there was no dearth of scrabbling rats and other vermin to vie with feral cats and homeless dogs in search of food. This is the world into which our orphan child was born. And he was not alone. This era was notorious for the misuse of orphaned children. They survived by becoming very sly and devious. Few ever reached adulthood without having become adept at thievery. Their talents also included ingratiating themselves into lucrative situations and becoming part of a larger group of orphans.

With these facts in mind, we begin our saga.

Chapter I

S he had never really been able to get used to the alley stench that assaulted her when the inevitable arose that she must open the back door to pitch out the kitchen refuse. Abigail could be assured of hearing the scrabbling of dogs, cats, and the large overfed rats. Thus, she stepped out only as far as absolutely necessary to be able to fling the offal as far away from the doorway as possible.

As the potful of slop splattered across the narrow space, she was horrified to witness a ragged urchin rise to meet the spray in an unsuccessful attempt to avoid the greasy, gray garbage.

Abigail let out a high-pitched squeak of apology, being the kind and generous woman that she was. She dropped the bucket and reached out to grab the bony bag of rags, now even more stinking and filthy than before his hapless encounter.

"Whuts you doin 'ere, Luv?" Not pausing for an answer, she continued, "Where's yer folks?" She glanced futilely around for a moment, then said, "C'mon in to th' storeroom, un letsus git yer wiped off a bit."

Tugging the rebellious chap toward the open doorway, Abigail's grip was like a band of iron against the pitiful arm of the scruffy lad. Not to be reckoned with, she would not be stayed from her course of action in dealing with the object of her concern. Never taking into account that the urchin was already—before the recent encounter with the kitchen garbage—stinking and filthy, she was only concerned with righting the wrong done to the poor boy. She'd get to the heart of his matter after she'd done the nearly impossible—getting him cleaned up.

"'Ere, now! Sit yerself atop this barrel." Lifting him with ease, she plopped his bony hide where she could get a decent look at him beneath the lantern hanging just above his shagged mop of hair. "Jeez, boy, who'se had ahold uv you? We can see th' answer to thatun, arlright! Nobuddy. That's who. Nobuddy! Son, ain't you got no folks atall?"

Not expecting an answer from her charge, Abigail quickly turned and grabbed an iron-bound oak bucket that caused the boys eyes to bulge in fear.

Water! Lor' hep me! he thought.

Pouring a copious amount into an iron pot, Abigail slung a coarse, brown chunk of hemp sack into it and sloshed it back and forth until it was sufficiently drenched.

Holding his nape, she slathered the dripping fabric against his matted hair and across his clenched face. "Hol' still! Ye look like a drowned rat. But we'll soon change that." No amount of dodging could stay her determined assault. Within a few seconds the tattered shirt was on the sod floor and being trod upon by this strong woman.

Without so much as a deep breath, she untied the cord from his waist and whipped away what modesty he had left. "Aaarrrgh!" he cried. "Ain't che got no manners? What's a man to do?"

Guffawing deeply, she threw back her head and howled in laughter. "Man? Ye be that only by God's grace, young'un. We inten's on using your arse in labor here at *The Cross and Fly*, we does. Me own boy left us not a for'night back. Leavin' w'out a word of g'bye, mind ya. Me'n Eddie been knowin' for the longes' that Boyd 'ud soon get his balls tight 'nouf to pull him away to other places. Bein'as how he's gone we could use 'elp here if'n I can decide you ain't got nobuddy else what's looking fer ye."

Suddenly, finding his voice amid his nakedness, he opened his mouth and let his brain lead his tongue. "I fled frum th' orphanage some days back, I guess. They sent me out wifout no funds to get some turnips fer th' stew. I was supposed to git 'em wifout gettin' caught. But since I didn't have nothing to carry 'em in, I just took one and was eatin' on it when I heard the vendor shoutin' that he wus missing his biggest show turnip and to git everbody looking for someone wif it. I figured it'd be better in the gutter than in my hand, so I pitched it under a passing coach. Since then I've been eatin' outa garbage barrels, or in alleyways behind places like this'un." And without so much as drawing in a breath, he continued. "An' I ain't agoin' back to th' devilish place, neither. Ye' cain't make me. I'll run off agin and agin, Miss."

Drawing into himself to appease the shakes, he was aware that the woman was smiling broadly as she toweled his body dry and brushed his unkempt hair with her hands. "What's I'm gonna put on, miss?"

"Don't you worry about that none. We'll soon have ye decked out in some of Boyd's leftovers. Only thing I'm wonderin' is if his shoes'll fitcha. We'll serve that when we can. Now, see here. Whut's yer name, son?"

"I don't rightly know, miss. They called me 'Hey boy,' and somehow I knew it was me."

"Did you have a mum what give ye up, or what?"

"Never knew a mum. Mr. Osbourne called her whore, and said I was a foundlin'... whatever that is."

"I see. Well, that bit o' information suits us right well. For the time bein' you're to answer to 'Rat,' and that with a big letter R! Won't have no disrespect in this establishment." Fitting his slight body with some rather fulsome pants, drawn up snug with the dirty cord that came from his castoffs, she pulled a full grey shirt over all that fell nearly to his knees.

"Now, Rat, you'll call me Missus Abigail..." As she turned, she slipped a crate to one side to expose a small dank room in the back corner of the storage room. Turning to swing her ample arm toward the opening, she proudly announced, "And this'll be yer private room whilst ye're wif us. There's a cot that's right cozy, I'm told, and a candle by it on the floor. After yer finished work in *The Cross and Fly*, ye can bring a straw light back for yer candle so's it'll be more like home, ye know."

"Yessum, Missus Abigail." Smiling to expose rotten and missing teeth, Rat felt a push of something akin to joy inside his emaciated soul.

"Come, now. Mr. Cavendish will be thinkin' I've dropped off the edge, and the crowd will be surgin' in 'afore long and there's plenty to keep us hoppin'."

Entering the hot kitchen, Rat was nearly knocked prone by the smells and permeating heat from the great fireplaces and food-laden wooden tables. Two hefty women were pouring and stirring and lifting and piling all sorts of heavenly viands. He felt sure this place would fully embrace his needs,... even those he'd yet to discover.

Looking beyond the kitchen toward the heavy brown curtain, he knew that on the other side must be the great room where the foods were served up. He felt Missus Abigail's hand at his back, shoving him forward toward the curtain. *I'm fearing to see whuts in there*, he thought.

•   •   •

Eddie Cavendish watched a small insurgence of assorted souls filing into his large public room. As his head serving girl was headed back to the kitchen, he turned quickly toward her. "Maggie, git yer missus! She oughta been back by now! Find 'er. We're fillin' fast and she's needed yesterdy."

At that moment Abigail brought her ample self forward while pushing something scraggly and gray and stumbling before her. She shoved her way past Maggie and pushed the boy toward Eddie, into the cooler interior of the large public room of *The Cross and Fly*. In the smoky mist of the open room, one could see there were several sailors, as well as a couple of dandies, seated at various tables.

Charging ahead, Mistress Abigail brought the young boy behind the high bar toward her husband. By way of introduction, she simply said, "The Lor' has favored us with a boy whut'll help take Boyd's place for awhile."

Glancing askance at the small frame bearing large gray eyes beneath a tussle of nondescript brown hair, he boomed, "Set 'im to trundlin' the used platters and mugs back to Mary fer washin'. Now! We're in need of fresh servin' pieces for the ones'll be headin' in soon. Need to keep ahead!"

Abigail swatted the bony rump as she shoved him into the common room. She watched as he approached the first table. "Ya finished wi' yer stew, mister? I'd be a takin' yer empty dish back...... Or, maybe ye'd like a tad more? And a chunk of bread to finish off?"

"Well, now, me good fella. Answer me this. What'll a 'tad more' cost me? Huh? Tell me quick, now."

Taking a trembling breath, and remembering all the times no one at the orphanage was allowed a second helping, Rat spoke from his heart. "Why, sir, for just a tad more and a small chunk o' bread the cost will be nothing, because the good man and lady of *The Cross and Fly* want their customers to be full and satisfied when they leave this place."

Throwing back his head with such force that his greasy black hair flew straight back, but quickly recovered its previous nestling against the overlarge and ornately embroidered collar, the man roared with laughter. "Glory be! A more generous offer I've never received, and I'll sure not deny you the opportunity o' supplyin' just a tad more o' that steamy stew, and a chunk o' Missus Abigail's excellent bread, son!" Lifting the empty bowl toward Rat, he continued, "Now tell ole' Tom yer name, boy!"

Without so much as batting an eyelid, the lad replied, "Rat, sir, I'm called Rat an' it's wif a Big Aaargh, I'm told."

"By Jove, my good man. That name alone will earn ye an extra pittance. To live to such a ripe old age as ye yerself have done is testament enough that such a moniker is proof of yer backbone!"

He held his hand out to the boy, and Rat looked at it uncomprehendingly. Glancing into the eyes of the gentleman, he spoke, "Whut's ye need, Mister?"

"Why! Your handclasp of friendship and understanding. Ain't ye never had a clasp afore?"

"Nossir. Can't say as I have." And then brightening, he spoke up and confessed, "But I've 'ad plenny o' cuffs to me head with fisted hands back at the place where I wuz livin' afore 'ere, sir."

With heartfelt understanding of the plight of many unwanted gutter children scrabbling to keep body and soul together, Tom said, "Well, here now. Take me bowl to the kitchen for that extra 'elpin' o' stew and that warm chunk o' bread so's I can finish off me meal. We'll talk more later on. Don't want yer Boss Man to be lookin' sidewise at ye' an' thinkin' yer sluffin' off yer labors t'day, now do we?"

Quickly, Rat hurried through the curtain into the warm kitchen. Handing the bowl to a perspiring maid busily ladling up the stew from a large black cauldron that was swinging over the glowing ashes within the huge fireplace, he said, "A gent'man needs just a tad more o' stew, if you please, ma'am."

Turning to smile at the lad, Judith took the bowl and ladled a generous amount into it and handed it back to the urchin. "Don't fergit to grab a small chunk o' bread from the basket by the curtain as ye' go back into the big room, and when ye gits back ye' tell me whut Master Eddie says about them extra 'elpin's?"

Nodding deeply, but concentrating on getting back to the table without spilling one drop, Rat shuffled through the dividing curtain. Keeping his attention on exactly where he was headed, he never glanced in the direction of Master Eddie.

"'Ere's yer extra helpin', sir, wif a mite o' bread too."

"Aye, Lad! And ye've just earned yersef an extra farthin' to add to yer generosity!"

Bobbing his scraggly mop to the man, Rat turned to see Master Eddie glaring at him beneath furrowed brows. *Suppose I oughta asked afore I offered the extra 'elpin'. 'Ope he don't box me ears!*

"C'm 'ere!" Eddie motioned with a crooked finger to Rat. "Now!" Leaning down to get face to face with his new employee, Eddie said, "Don't never offer extra anything without checkin' with the cooks afore hand... Y'e see son, you 'n' me out 'ere, we don't egzakly know how much the cooks got back there. They know 'ow many they'll feed for the evenin', but we don't. Ye was lucky tonight, though. Appears there wuz enough for yer friend, but just suppose there wuzzen'. Now whut d'ye spose woulda been yer excuse back to him after ye'd dun offered the extra? Huh?"

"Master Eddie, I'm very sorry! I ain't got no scuses about it. I jus' never give it a thought."

"Yep, son, now that's the rub. Thought! Ye've gotta develop yer thought processes, now don't yer know!" Raising himself back upright, Eddie stuck out his opened palm and said, "I'll just take that farthin' ye got... 'twill hep ye with yer thought processes beginnin' now."

• • •

Rat considered himself very blessed (if he was able to ken such a condition) to be where he had ended up. With folks that cared about his welfare (if he knew what that meant), and where he had a warm place to rest his frail body and belch his satisfying meals.

Inexorably time marched on, and Rat grew smarter in his thought processes as well as in his physical body. The more he began to explore his surroundings, the more he began to realize he was somewhat of an asset to *The Cross and Fly*.

Mistress Abigail often trusted him to foray into the Saturday market with money in hand to purchase needed supplies. His name became known by the merchants and they often held back the vegetables they knew he'd be looking for. One such vendor happened to be Master Oldfield, seller of fine purple-top turnips.

The first time Rat came face to face with the gentleman, his thought processes pulled up his memory of that lovely turnip he'd stolen. *Firs' chance I gits to pay for that turnip, I will. I can pay for the amount of turnips for the kitchen, then I'll jes put one of 'em back in his pile... No! That'll be like stealin' from Master Eddie. I cain't do that. Boy! My thought processes is workin' too much. I'll need to process this'un sum more.*

That night on his cot in the little room at the back of the storeroom, Rat tackled his problem of how he'd repay the turnip vendor for the stolen vegetable. But sleep soon overcame his ponderings, and Rat rested deeply.

•   •   •

Approaching the turnip vendor, Rat had great misgivings concerning his plan to obtain the cost of a large turnip. Rat stood just off to one side to scan the offerings to try to locate a turnip that came close to the size of the one he'd pilfered.

Several years had passed and Rat felt sure that the vendor would never suspect him of having been the turnip thief. Finding the aproned gentleman without a current customer, Rat stepped forward to catch the man's attention. "Sir, what would that lovely turnip right there," as he pointed, "be costin' me if I could afford to buy it, sir? Please."

Harrumphing, and becoming serious with thought, he answered, "Me boy, thetunw'd be a 'hapenny and no less." But he quickly continued, "But if'n ye'd like enou' fer a potful… say five 'r six, I'd make ye a deal for two pence."

Without blinking an eye, Rat came back with, "Sir, I'd sure love to buy that big one, but seein' as how I ain't got a jingle o' coin to my name, I'm thinking that what if ye'd have a little somethin' needin' doin' around here where I might earn enou' ter buy just that big, purty one. Would ye think on it, sir? I'm purty strong and would do yer biddin' fer that turnip, sir."

"Bein' as how I sees ye'r a industrious sorta lad, I might find somethin' fer ye. It's too close to shuttin' down time now, but come back next week and see if I can use yer help."

Rat turned to leave when he heard the vendor speak. "Wait, son, come back. Yer can help me right now to sort out and store up and fold up me stand. I think that much would be payment enough for that great turnip." And the man reached out to hand the beautiful turnip into Rat's hands.

Rat quickly laid it back amidst its kind and said, "Sir, kind sir, I'll help you first; then when we're finished, we'll settle about that turnip, sir."

"Thank 'ee kindly, young man. Ye're a rare one if ever I seen one, son." Turning, he said, "Come quickly and fetch the empty crates from beneath the table. Store as many as you can in each one. Now careful, don't drop 'em... Nestle 'em easy now."

With great care and efficiency, Rat and the vendor worked side by side to stow the produce and to lift the crates onto a wheeled cart that had been unseen from the street side. "Will ye be back next market day, sir?"

"If'n God's willin' I shall. Me'n the goodwife been working this market fer nigh on ten years."

"D'ye have a plot o' land nearby, sir?"

With a smart nod, "Inherited from th' wife's da when he passed on. Provided fer his family and now mine, but it do take a mite o'work. Ye canno' be a slug-a-bed and 'spect to make a livin', I c'n tell ye that right now."

"I hope never to be one 'er them, sir. I sure feels we all mus' make our way as soon as we're able, don't yer think?"

"Why, lad, yer got a good head 'pon them skinny shoulders. Someday, I'll vow, ye'll be sumbuddy! Mark my word."

They had everything neatly stowed, the street swept, the loose boards of the stand knocked down and folded over the top of the turnip crates, and all covered with the canvas drape. As the vendor turned to reach for the lovely turnip that he'd placed in the front corner of the cart so as to be easily reached, Rat held his arm back. Looking directly into the questioning eyes of the vendor, he said, "Sir, please, sir, keep that lovely turnip. Yer see, I stole a turnip from your stand some years back, and that deed has cost me much guilt an' loss of contentment. The work I done fer ye t'day is my way to try to pay for my sins a'gin' ye, and ask fer yer fergiv'ness." Rat's eyes were filled with tears as big as any the vendor had ever seen. They broke over his lower lashes to streak through the dust and dirt of Rat's upturned face.

Stooping somewhat to enfold the strong, young body within his huge arms, the vendor said, "Me boy, yer fergiv'n, and what I said about yer bein' sumbuddy special, well, I meant it. Now, give it no more thought. I'd be honored if ye'd come around a'gin to help me break down for the day. I'll give ye yer choict of any turnip on my shelf." And with that he gave Rat a snug hug and a swat on his butt to send him off.

Running down the cobblestones, Rat looked back to wave to the vendor and thought, *I never even asked him his name. I'll do it next time.*

.   .   .

Bounding through the storage room door of *The Cross and Fly*, he skidded to a quick stop as Missus Abigail swung through from the kitchen. "Where've ye been, boy? We been worried sick about ye!"

"I'm sorry, I tole Master Eddie I had an errand to run at market. Wuz I gone too long, miss?"

"Yes! A hour is too much time away. Yer know yer needed here, Rat. Ye haf ta work fer yer livin'. Now, git in the big room and start tappin' ale."

Rat made it his quest to please Master Eddie as best as he could, knowing his station to be one of splendor compared to what it was before he happened to find refuge in Missus Abigail's alley.

His frail frame had grown and waxed strong, as much by laborious tasks as by the generous victuals provided by the cooks of *The Cross and Fly*.

.   .   .

While admiring the silent efficiency with which Rat was going about his labors, Eddie suddenly became aware that the boy had been with them… what? Four, maybe five years now. With keen reckoning, Master Eddie decided it was past time to figure out a date of birth for Rat, as well as come up with a suitable name for the lad. Getting this information down onto some sort of official paper was the real drawback. Eddie considered putting his concerns into the capable hands of one of his best customers, Squire Petrie. As soon as the squire found his way down to the docks again, and deigned to visit for a pint and some of the better foods consistently offered by *The Cross and Fly*, Eddie figured he'd enlist his help to do what he could for the lad.

If Rat was to ever be allowed to advance from his sour beginnings, he'd need to be armed with more of a moniker than the one at present, and some official papers to offer as proof of his heritage. With the help of Missus Abigail, they came up with a formula for estimating Rat's age. You see, when the lad had first appeared, they saw he was still sporting baby teeth, at least the ones not rotten to gum level. He had to have been somewhere around five and a few months. Soon after his taking up residence at *The Cross and Fly*, a full-grown lower front tooth pushed through, shoving away the rotten rim of a baby tooth. Just a few short days later another next to it became loosened and was pulled out forthwith, opening the way for his second lower front tooth to emerge.

Armed with this knowledge, Rat's surrogate parents enlisted the help of Squire Petrie some few days later. The friendly squire produced a crumpled paper from his breast pocket, and found the stub of a string-wrapped sliver of graphite from inside his tricorn. Laboriously he took all the information provided, and soon listed the date of birth as the twenty-first day of September in the year of our Lord, 1824. With this information handy, they pushed forward to the year they were presently living, 1835. This cyphering would make Rat soon to be eleven years old. He'd been with them now for five years coming the Fall Equinox. Wanting Rat to experience advancement with honest folks, Eddie prompted the squire to keep a live eye out for an opportunity to present itself on behalf of Rat.

"Afore he's let out to work for his livin', I'd like you to help us procure a decent name for the chap. Got any ideas, Squire?"

"Let me think on it for a few days. Sure we can come up with something to give the boy a proper sendoff into the world, what!"

Just as their son Boyd had been pulled away, the proprietors of *The Cross and Fly* certainly understood the pull of the world outside their doors upon Rat. Trying to hold him to his security with them would come to naught, they knew. No need pretending that Rat would be with them much longer. Consequently, both Eddie and Abigail had their eyes open to opportunities of finding a new boy to help out in their lucrative operation.

In fact, they approached the women that labored in the kitchens to also maintain some attention toward that end. Within a fortnight, Mary sent word to Mr. Eddie that her niece, Margerie Anne had a by-blow from her mistress's son not long ago past. The babe was sent to be raised by his father's valet's daughter in Chesshire. They say he's a right bonnie lad and might be just the right one to be fostered by the proprietors of *The Cross and Fly*.

Without much ado, the boy was sent for on a trial basis while Rat was still the favored son. As soon as Canton was ushered into the presence of the Cavendishes, Rat welcomed him with a toothsome grin. Having recalled exactly how terribly 'out of place' he'd felt upon being thrust into this place, Rat was as determined as possible to help his coworker become comfortable.

Tapping on Missus Abigail's shoulder, Rat looked into her intelligent eyes and asked, "Where'm I to sleep now, Ma'am?"

Smiling at the boy of her heart, "Now ye need not worry none, Rat. We've had another comfy bed placed by yourn. Ye'll have nice company fer awhile."

Relieved at this news, Rat shook hands with Canton, and welcomed him to T*the Cross and Fly*. "Best place for us in all this world. And I'll take it upon meself to be a'teachin' you what ye need to know to keep y'r master and missus and all the good customers of this 'stablishmint happy." Rat spoke gently to this new son.

"Take charge now, Rat, and show young Canton where he'll be sleepin'. And all the necessaries he'll be lookin' for, too. Then you bring him right back here."

Rat, taking hold of Canton's hand, led the boy into the back, but did pause just long enough to show him the cooks of the kitchen.... "Miss Mary, Miss Maggie, 'n Miss Judith, there." Entering the storage room he invited Canton into their private chamber. Since Rat had been there for a number of years, he'd made the cave somewhat more agreeable. With his own money, he'd bought a real oil lamp to set on a sturdy crate he'd begged from Mr. Oldfield, the turnip seller. Religiously, Rat had kept the sod floor somewhat warmer by the addition of straw confiscated from the fields after threshing.

Finally, the newcomer found his tongue and said, "Awww, I wanna go home!"

Taken somewhat aback, Rat slipped one arm over Canton's shoulder and hugged him to his side. "Ye'll be arrite, Canton. It'll take ye jes a small while til ye'll be struttin' aroun' like ye own this place! Jes you wait'nsee. Why, y'r so much better off than I wuz when Missus Abigail found me. I was sleepin' in crates, and fightin' with th' animals for sumptin to eat! Ye don't yet ken how wonderful it is here compared to ever'where else ye could end up."

Snuffling and swiping an arm across his eyes, he turned to Rat, "Where'd you come from?"

"Nobuddy knows. An' that's a truff, it is." Puffing out his chest some little bit, Rat continued, "I was a foundlin', I wuz. But onct I was rescued here, I wuz given a real name whut begins wif a capital Arrr."

"I never heard of anybody with such a name as yours, Rat. Don't it make you feel bad?"

"No! No... It's that capital Arrr what makes the difference. I never have felt ashamed of it. I think it says I'm somebuddy what's special. Now, let's us git back to the Big Room, and git to work. We got's lots to do afore bedtime. You just do what I do and what I say, arright?"

"Sure, Rat."

The new help was working out fine. After a few days of despondency, ably cured by Rat's intervention, Canton soon found his footing and was worthy of every meal and the lodging provided.

Chapter II

S quire Petrie was greeted by Eddie as he entered the Big Room with Captain Witherspoon. The men were seated at the best table at the front window which looked out over the quay, where the Captain's trade ship *Narcissus* was tethered.

Pushing back their chairs, and lighting a couple of the cigars newly-brought from Cuba, the men sat in companionable silence until the Captain harrumphed gently and said, "Guido, I find myself in dire need of a good cabin boy. The lad what was with me for nigh on three years up and left before I could get around to promoting him. Keep this quest in mind as you go about the area, would you?"

"Certainly, I shall. About what age would you be preferrin'?"

"Oh, somewhere around 10 to 12 is best. Boys of that age have usually learned enough to be able to follow orders sufficient to please most anyone. They ought to've had a fairly rough life to overcome and so be the stronger for it."

About that time, Rat and Canton were seen busily wiping down the chairs and tables in anticipation of the patrons expected for the evening meal. The smells emanating from the kitchens were simply mouth-watering. The two friends watched the boys without curiosity for a while, then both glanced at each other with a smile.

"Do you suppose the goodman of this establishment would be willing to part with the elder of those boys, Squire?"

"As a matter of fact, I know that he would. Not but a few days back he instructed me to try to locate a good position for the boy, as he's been such a blessing to his master, and so he doesn't desire to hold the lad back from a good life."

"Fine! I'll speak to Master Cavendish as soon as we've partaken of our meal. I can declare, the odours from the kitchen will set a man's stomach to filling with anticipation. Whatever it is a'cookin' must surely be scrumptious."

"Rat, Canton, here! Now!"

Scrambling to get to their master as fast as possible, the boys hurried toward the high bar. "Yessir, yessir, Master Eddie," they parroted together.

Leaning over somewhat to speak, he said, "Gent'men, hie y'rsef's over to the table by the front window where Squire Petrie is sittin' with the Sea Captain. Take their order for vittles and see that they are served quickly, now. Careful, no spillin', no trippin neither. Now go."

Striding quickly to the front window table, Rat said to his cohort, "Now you jes keep quiet; I'll do the talkin', but you help me do the listening. Arright?"

"Sure, Rat."

"Good ev'nin', gent'men. If'n you're ready we'll give you the bill o' fare."

Smiling, the two men nodded as Rat spieled off the list of foods he'd seen coming off the stoves and out of the huge open fireplaces.

"To begin wif, sirs, we has the best of all breads. They be hefty to sop up ever bit o' broth whut might be left from yer meal." And he continued with a list of all that he remembered from the cooks' labors. Then he added, "But I gotta tell you thet there ain't much in the way o' sweets. The fruits what wuz laid by is all gone, and it'll be some while before any fresh is found 'round here."

"Now that's a right hefty list of foods ye've given us, young man. Just what would you suggest we begin with for our repast?" asked Squire Petrie.

"Well, since ye be askin', I'd suggest the roasted beef wif pataters and gravy. Miss Judith makes th' bes' in all th' world!" said Rat, grinning broadly.

"Then, 'pon my word, that's what we'll have. The captain and I shall be a'waitin' with bated breath for you to get it out here, young sir."

Turning to hurry back toward the kitchen, Rat reached for Canton's hand and pulled him along.

Squire Petrie spoke quickly to Captain Witherspoon. "Yer searching is over, my good man. I do believe that young Rat is exactly what ye maybe looking fer in a cabin boy. What do ye think?"

"Seems rather intelligent and especially industrious. Do you think the master will part with him?"

"I'm sure. In fact, as I already told you, he's asked me to be on the alert for some good position for Rat, being as how he's of an age to begin his career in life."

"Good, I'll speak to the master as soon as we've eaten. He'll give some indication as to whether or not he thinks this boy will take to the sea or no."

• • •

Within a fortnight, Rat found himself, for the first time, aboard a ship. Since he had no idea of any personal knowledge of the sea, he was simply filled with excitement. Captain Witherspoon had seen him outfitted with the few clothes he'd need, assuring Rat that new ones could be made or purchased as needed and not until.

Rat's dearest possessions, presented to him by Captain Witherspoon, were a newly carved seaman's chest and a seaman's sewing packet. Having been forewarned that he'd learn to not only mend but also make items of clothing for himself, and possibly for the Captain. He swelled with pride in this knowledge…, never doubting these events would come to pass.

Mr. Flakton was assigned to instruct Rat in duties of service to the captain, as well as to safety. Rat was determined to never need to be told a second time in any service or instruction. He was going to keep his thought processes on steady ahead. *Aboard this ship*, Rat thought to himself, *I've found my place in life now. My destiny is fulfilled!*

Leaving the London Port was wonderful! Watching Missus Abigail waving with all her might was beautiful. Suddenly, tears sprang, unwanted but unavoidable, and rolled down his cheeks. A lump rose in his throat and left him totally unable to swallow. The weight of his situation almost overcame his determination to prove himself to be a man…, ready for the life of a man. Rising to his toes, he whipped off his neck scarf and waved it mightily for her to see the joy he did not feel.

He waved until she was but a speck. He turned to find Mr. Flakton watching him. And so began his new career as a seaman.

• • •

Within a few short, sick weeks, Rat found his sea legs and was able to get the captain's meals served while they were still relatively hot. Every minute was filled with work or lessons. He never realized that men of the sea were such independent souls. They could do anything and everything. ., from mending sails to making leather shoes—which they never wore aboard ship. Mostly the crew went barefoot for a better foothold on the deck.

During the quiet time of meals, the captain taught Rat cyphering and reading and writing. Rat was even privy to watch as the daily log was written. He was also told that in the event of piracy the log was to be stowed into a heavily-weighted case and cast into the sea by the first man that could take hold of it.

Very few events took place that were not fully expected, and precautions were taken to alleviate the problems before they hardly took hold. Rat became adept at anticipating, and thereby was found to be very worthy and useful.

From the time he boarded the *Narcissus* to the time they first docked at port, Rat was advancing his thought processes at a very rapid rate. Upon landing at Singapore, Captain Witherspoon sent for him to come immediately. Shimmying down the rigging and bouncing across the spotless deck, he ran.

"Rat, I believe the hour has finally arrived when you must begin wearing the mantle of a true and mature man. Master Cavendish informed me that he'd never gotten around to pronouncing a new name upon you, and I would like to be the one accomplish this on your behalf. Now is the time we must assign a new name for you to assume for the remainder of your life."

"Why do you think I'd be needin' another name, sir?" asked Rat.

"My good man, the moniker placed upon your child's body has served you well. That is, up until now. It is now expedient for you to claim a more profound name for yourself. One in which you can be truly proud, and that speaks well of your past." Settling himself into his chair, Captain Witherspoon pulled forth across his desk several important-appearing documents, and proceeded to dip the nib of his plume into the inkwell. "Now I've given a great deal of thought into this new name of yours. Let's see if the sound of it lays well upon your own ears, shall we?"

"Sure, sir, I think this is kinda' exciting. What's the name ye've come up with?"

"Seeing as how you are presently named 'RAT,' I considered the using of those three letters for your forever-name. What do you think of Ryan for the 'R.' Alexander for the 'A.' Trenton for the 'T.' Your new name would be Ryan Alexander Trenton. How does that suit you?"

"Ryan Alexander Trenton. Ryan Alexander Trenton. Why, I think that sounds really nice. You don't suppose folks will think I'm from some fine line o' lords and ladies, do ye?"

"Ryan, what other people think or don't think, ought never affect what you know about your own self. Never let another human being define who or what you are. You alone hold your destiny within yourself." Nodding, Captain Witherspoon went on, "The only Being you need ever be swayed by is the Good Lord Almighty. And He's always got the first and last word about your path in life. Do all in your power to please Him and you'll go far."

Entering the birthdate arrived at by the owners of *The Cross and Fly*, as being September 21, 1824, and carefully writing the new name upon two lines of the official documents, Captain Witherspoon sent for the quartermaster, Mr. Flackton. As soon as he entered the captain's quarters, he was handed the documents for perusal and then asked to sign as witness to the event. After it was done, a red wax seal was dripped upon the parchment and the heavy signet ring on the forefinger of the captain's left hand was pressed into the warm wax and carefully lifted off, leaving the cooling wax to evidence the important and official documents.

One document was carefully rolled and inserted into a sturdy, leather tube with a tight-fitting lid, for total protection. Handing the tube over to Ryan, the captain said, "You guard this with your life. Once you leave this ship for another career you will be called upon to prove exactly who you are. This document will hold fast in any court of law for any circumstance, as it carries the signatures of both the quartermaster of the *Narcissus* and that of her captain. The other will be sent to London for filing and safekeeping on your behalf."

Turning to rise from his chair, he continued, "Get dressed, Ryan; we're going ashore for a few days. We're in here for offloading our hold, and total cleaning and repairs are needed. Then we'll be loading some very rare and beautiful stock for the Americas."

•　　•　　•

Having been with Captain Confidence J. Witherspoon for just over eleven years, and attaining the rank of First Mate, Mister Ryan was a man to be reckoned with. Standing well over six feet, with an abundance of thick chestnut hair that waved and curled over his scalp, with sparkling gray eyes beneath drawn brows and fringed with thick black lashes, he stood with powerful legs spread for stability as the *Narcissus* pitched this way and that. Shouting orders to the crew to hold true to course, he knew the wind would soon turn. The swirling clouds overhead portended such, and he was secure in his assessment of the outcome.

Mister Lassiter, ship's pilot, was in complete agreement with his first mate. Captain Witherspoon was abed in his cabin; had been for nigh on to a week, with some malady the surgeon could not put his finger on. Consequently, no matter what was plied into him, nothing was alleviating his problems. Everyone was called upon to pray for their captain's speedy recovery. No one prayed deeper than did Mister Ryan. He did not relish his position at this point in time. He'd much rather be taking his orders from his captain.

Finally, Surgeon Osbourne decided to concoct a purge. Hoping the cleansing would rid the captain's body of the offending disease without killing him, he began gathering the dried herbs and leaves he'd stowed in his well-guarded satchel to grind into a potent powder. Without any idea as to how much he may or may not need, he proceeded to stir a hefty spoonful into watered brandy. Lifting his captain's head from the damp pillow, he began to dribble the concoction across his lips and watched as his gullet moved up and down with each swallow. As soon as every drop was down his throat, Mr. Osbourne began to pray. "Lord God, please let this do the trick. Let our good captain overcome whatever this sickness is. Amen."

Suddenly the ship pitched so violently that Captain Witherspoon was literally cast out onto the floor of his cabin with a bounding thud. Mr. Osbourne was awestruck, and watched in abject horror as a forceful spewing came forth from the mouth of his captain and was flung clear across the room. The odour of the vomitus was terrible.

Mr. Osbourne bounded up the steps and onto the mid-deck, screaming for help. "Bring mops! Bring sloshing water! Bring Mr. Trenton! Now! Quick! Captain's in need of help!" And he disappeared back down the steps.

"She's in your hands, Mr. Lassiter," shouted Ryan, as he turned to run toward the mid-deck and the captain's quarters. Bounding down into the cabin, the smell nearly overcame him. With eyes wide and questioning, he asked, "What's that?"

"His sickness. That's it. Look here. I've found the problem. A critter of extraordinary length and with a ferocious mandible what was sucking the life from Captain Witherspoon! And from the size of it, I do fear there may be eggs or offspring still in his intestines. As soon as he's able, I'll need to give him another draft of the purge and hope it'll stay down long enough for some of it to go all the way through and clean anything else out. But I do believe now we've got him on the mend."

Three of the crew were busy cleaning and mopping the floor. The windows were opened, allowing the salt spray to cleanse the room of the vile odours. Ryan and Dr. Osbourne had stripped the sick man and were cleaning him up before redressing him into fresh bedclothes. "We'll need to pack him in plenty of rags that we can dispose of overboard. If my purge does what I want, then he'll not have any control over his bowels. He'll need one of us with him at all times. Will you stand with me, sir?"

"Never doubt it. This man is like a father to me. I'd walk through fire for him, sir. You just tell me what you want me to do, then consider it done," replied Ryan.

•   •   •

Seeing Captain Confidence Witherspoon up and about—albeit moving somewhat slow and gingerly—was a boost to his crew. During the worst of the passage First Mate Ryan has proved his prowess, as Captain Witherspoon knew he would. The *Narcissus* had rounded Cape Horn, literally at the bottom of the world, through high seas and dangerous tides, with no loss of crew or stowage. They were headed to the port of San Francisco, which was an excitement for everyone aboard.

The *Narcissus* had been off loaded in the Port of New York, cleaned, repaired, and loaded with as much lumber and building supplies as could possibly be stowed. A veritable building boom was causing a dire need for such supplies as could be brought as often as possible. Top dollar was expected and so the bay was overcrowded, thereby causing the opposite to occur. Supplies sometimes rotted while still aboard ships stuck in the harbor. Thieves confiscated what they could lay their claws on to sell to the highest bidder on the black markets. The port was notorious for malefactors. The *Narcissus* had sailed unawares into the eye of a storm of evil-doers in San Francisco.

The Narcissus had left New York harbor just eight weeks ago when Captain Witherspoon became ill. Nearly eight weeks later they'd sailed around the Horn and were on the last leg of the journey as he was recuperating. By the time they finally found berth in San Francisco, after a six months' trip, he was in fairly good health. As the crew left ship for a well-earned leave, Captain Witherspoon, First Mate Ryan A. Trenton, and the Saw-Bones Osbourne found their way inland to a hostelry.

Ryan had been in exotic ports, seen plenty of unusual sights, and experienced foods of unexpected flavors, but this San Francisco was unique to all he'd ever seen. There was such a variety of people. All the folks of other worlds were landed here. He'd not need to travel anywhere else to view the myriad casts of people. They were all right here, and he realized deep within his thought processes there were plenty of dangers mixed in with the benign. Dealing with anyone would be a challenge.

The *Narcissus* would be down for cleaning and repairs after being divested of her goods. The ship would be ready to reload in as few as three months. Knowing many of the men of his crew would find other employment before then, the captain began immediately to hire on as many hands as he could find that would be willing to assume the varied duties needed aboard ship. Mr. Osbourne had assured him that he could be counted on to maintain his duties once more aboard the *Narcissus*. Likewise, Ryan also said he'd like to stay on. So go the best laid plans of mice and men.

Chapter III

S everal weeks later the men were seated at a well-laid table in the hotel dining room. Ryan, Osbourne, and Captain Witherspoon were quietly discussing the itinerary for publishing to entice needed seamen to apply for the upcoming departure of the *Narcissus*. She was partially loaded with dried foods and barrels of staples for the crew. Enough to get them to their next destination —from the Port of San Francisco to Cuba—where the filling of the hold would be completed by the loading of Cuban tobaccos headed for Europe.

Thus far the hiring was going well. Captain Witherspoon felt that by the end of another couple of weeks they'd have a full roster of seaman to man the ship.

Sitting well back into the overstuffed chairs, soaking in the variety scenes to take hold of one's' attention, even within such a confined area as that of the lobby and dining room, the three men were beginning to nod into their respective snifters of Napoleon Brandy, when a finely dressed elderly gentleman strode purposefully up to their table.

Rousing quickly, the trio sat upright, then stood as one. Reaching forward with a friendly hand, the man took the captain's in his own and shook it firmly.

"Forgive this untimely interruption, sirs. But I find myself in dire need of your expertise." Continuing, he went on, "My name is Horace Featherstone and I happen to be the procurer and distributor of great artistic items. I'd very much be honored if you'd be so kind as to visit, at your convenience to be sure, my nearby establishment. If you find your ship has room for some of the treasures to which I have access, to transport them to European ports and then upon your advancement to other splendid ports whereby you would purchase... Of course on my behalf, such oddities and artistic works as you would deem I'd have need of for my establishment. You would be well compensated for your troubles." Pausing, he looked at each man in turn.

Speaking first, Captain Witherspoon said, "I'm all for making money for my ship and crew. As for myself, I'd be happy to visit your establishment to glean some idea of your tastes and needs to offer the rare and odd treasures I feel you are seeking."

"Splendid! Would it be to your liking for us to hie to one of my warehouses now? It truly is nearby... just a quick walk. 'Twould give you an opportunity to acquaint yourselves with some of the town."

•　•　•

Leaving the lobby, the four men, led by Featherstone and Witherspoon, accompanied by Osbourne and Trenton stepping in behind them, entered the noise and bustle of the street.

The path taken led them into a maze of buildings, confusing and ill-planned. Trusting their leader, the men followed on into the deepening shadows and fog. Arriving at last, Mister Featherstone stopped at a wide building of weathered woods and rusted metals. Witherspoon knew they were near the docks by the smells and surrounding sounds. Featherstone keyed open two hefty locks to slide back double doors to a gaping black interior. Reaching inside to bring forth an oil lantern, he quickly lit it and held it high, lighting the interior enough to allow the men to enter surefootedly. Turning back he slid closed the doors and bolted them from the inside.

RAT

Captain Witherspoon asked, "Are the articles you wish us to see still contained within their crates, or are they displayed where I can get a good look at them?"

"By all means, sir, they are housed in the next room where they have been removed from their packing and displayed upon shelves for your observation. Come!"

The men advanced together, holding close to the light being held by Featherstone. Their steps rang out with echoes, denoting the emptiness of the area in which they presently walked. Witherspoon began to feel the hair rise on the nape of his neck. He did not like being so vulnerable, not having any control whatsoever of his surroundings. Finally, Featherstone reached and opened another door, and they entered a brightly lit room. Not nearly as large as the previous one, but, as promised, there were tables and shelves of assorted artifacts and decorative objects as well as oriental paintings. Witherspoon breathed easier now and glanced at his smiling host.

"As you now observe, Captain, what you see is only a small sample of the inventory contained in two other warehouses. I have purchased my stock mostly from the ships bringing Chinese migrants to this area. Many items were bartered for the cost of their passage."

"Just who do you expect to trade your collections to?" asked Captain Witherspoon.

Pausing to stroke an elaborately decorated porcelain vase, Featherstone said, "California is expanding faster than materials can be supplied. Migrants are pouring in by the hundreds. There's more available labor than jobs. But! The beauty of this quandary is that in the not too distant future the men made wealthy by this influx and opportunity will be clamoring for more than the bare essentials. They and their wives will fall over themselves to own such heady items as you see here. Their wealth will mean my wealth." Pausing only slightly, he continued, "And you, Witherspoon, and your fine ship's crew will also benefit greatly by continuing to stock my warehouses."

As the Captain and Osbourne continued to admire the exotic works housed within the large space, Ryan had walked around the room and

29

was admiring an exquisitely carved screen. Ryan suddenly smelled flowers. He stopped, turned, and spied a beautiful young girl in oriental dress smiling shyly at him. He returned her smile, and surprisingly she beckoned to him to come to her. Without hesitating, Ryan walked to where she was waiting beyond the carved screen. As he rounded the screen he saw her slip through a sliding door which she held aside for him to enter. She quickly slid it shut behind him and took his hand.

Ryan was aware that the odor of flowers was becoming overpowering as she quickly pulled him onward. Giving her no resistance, he allowed her lead, and when she stopped she motioned for him to sit on a low, pillowed couch. Ryan was feeling very heavy-headed as she gently shoved him to lie prone. He smiled as she tugged off his boots and loosened his wide belt.

. . .

"We must be getting back to our lodgings, Featherstone. Where did Master Ryan get off to? Do you have any idea?"

"Don't fret the young man. We have a wonderful Chinese family that has quarters beyond this display area. I feel sure the daughter, Mai Lin, has taken an interest in him and is showing him off to her family. He's more than likely enjoying their evening repast. I'll see to it that he's delivered back to your inn 'ere long."

Mr. Featherstone led the winding and confusing alleys back to his new business partners' lodging. To Witherspoon, it felt somehow a quicker trip than was the initial foray to the warehouse. Upon arrival, the men shook hands once again, and vowed to anticipate the next encounter with great expectations.

Next morning at breakfast Mr. Osbourne inquired as to the health of young Ryan. "Much to my consternation the boy has not yet made it back. Nor have I seen hide nor hair of our wealthy businessman!" spoke out Captain Witherspoon with quite a vengeance. "Immediately upon the completion of our breakfast, we must get back to that place where we were last evening. He'd better still be there, too! Hopefully, he's simply become engrossed with these new acquaintances and simply allowed himself to be deterred from his duty.

"Eat up Osbourne. We must needs to be about this business!"

• • •

No matter which street or alleyway the men travelled, no headway was realized in the locating of the particular warehouse. Several times they approached strangers to inquire as to the whereabouts of Mr. Featherstone's warehouses. The answers were consistently negative. No one along the quay had any knowledge of such a name or place—or else they all were sharing in the same lie.

After a fortnight of searching, Witherspoon and Osbourne agreed that the probability of Ryan being kidnapped and shanghaied was foremost. After the *Narcissus* was cleaned, repaired, and loaded with viands to hold the crew until Cuba, they set sail once more. Captain Witherspoon had been able to hire on a new crew and even to find a fairly capable first mate to take Ryan's place. He was especially grateful to find a young Chinese lad to be his Cabin Boy. The boy's name belied his strength and determination. His prostitute mother had tagged him with Blossom Twig because she avowed, "He came from my body red like quince blossom and skinny like twig!" Witherspoon recalled with tenderness young Rat who had become like a son to his heart. He'd taken the time and effort to bestow upon him a new name, and he'd do the same for Blossom Twig.

Marching along the clean deck boards with hands clasped behind his back, head somewhat bent, deep in thought, he prayed for the safety of Ryan and for God to help him raise up his new boy with honor and strength. *Let's see now, what might be an appropriate name for my new charge.*

Chapter IV

R yan slowly became aware of himself. Daring to open his eyes only enough to be able to peer through his lashes, he was astonished to realize he was blind. On second thought, maybe he was held in some dark place where no light was able to penetrate. Preferring the latter to the initial, he determined to mentally press into his body. *My rump seems wet... feet bare and cold... head heavy... hands not there! Oh my God! Someone has severed my hands! Wait, I think I can feel and move my shoulders. Ah, yes. Hands are tied. Feet too I suspect.* Moving his legs, his feet were pulled through wet mud. *Must be a dungeon or cave. I'm lying on damp earth, of that I'm sure.* Able to find his feet were not bound, he heavily shuffled his body to a sitting position. Panting with the exertion, he rolled his shoulders and nodded his head in an attempt to the get the blood flowing once again. He came to the conclusion that his only bindings were holding his hands behind his back. The needles of surging blood brought great relief and happiness. *At least the bonds aren't as tight as they could be.* Armed with this understanding, he fisted and opened his hands for several minutes, until he began to feel his nails digging into his palms.

Humping his kneeling body across, inch by inch, around his prison, he was able to estimate the space of his captivity to be about ten feet wide, but only the Lord knew how much the distance in the cross direction. After counting the shuffles in one direction without encountering a wall or barrier, he reversed himself with a like number of shuffles. He estimated he was near to being back where he'd begun. Thus, he continued in that way for all of fifty counts without barrier. *I have to be in a cave of some kind.*

Voices! *Oh my God, help me. Think! Think! I need to get back to where I was or they'll know I'm awake.* Forcing himself to remain calm, he attempted to locate the feel of the place where he'd awakened. Shuffling along in the blackness, he prayed for guidance. Finally, realizing the voices were getting nearer, he simply gave up and threw his body down upon his right side and closed his eyes. With great effort he slowed his breathing and calmed his pounding heart. Keeping his eyes opened only slightly, he was gratified to witness the wavering beams of light cast by lanterns held aloft by the men inescapably moving in his direction. Silently he thanked God that he wasn't blind.

"Hey! Lookie here boys! Our young Toadie's been awake some." Kicking at the backside of Ryan, the abuse brought forth a moan from the prisoner. "How're ye feelin', Master Ryan?" queried the unknown assailant. No benefit to be realized by pretending any longer, Ryan lifted his head just off the earth and said, "Where am I? Why am I here? Who are you?"

Hearing the raucous laughter of several men, Ryan estimated there were three or four occupying the cave with him. "Why, ye've been wanted by our boss to help him with some extra special endeavors!" More ridiculous laughter accompanied the statement. Ryan saw no humor in his situation.

"Will you help me to my feet? My body feels as though I've been bound to the keel in a storm!"

More laughter by his captors. "He's got a sense o'humor about him, he does. He'll be fun to train in his labors, won't he boys?" Arms went around his body, lifting him to a sitting position and then upward until he was able to get his legs and feet beneath. Dragging him to the side of the cave, they leaned him against the musty wall. "We'll be back and bring ye some vittles and wine. Boss wants ye in good condition."

RAT

"Boss? Boss? Who is this boss you speak of?"

"Why, ye sure don't need to know that. Just understand he has found ye to be necessary for something very special!" The men howled with more laughter. "Rest yer bones, boy. Ye'll need all yer strength to serve probably in some foreign hell hole!" And they laughed harder.

Daring to even open his mouth, Ryan asked, "Where are my boots and my belt? I need them, please."

More throaty laughter as they left him once more in the dead dark. "Now don't ye go nowhere boy. We'll be back before ye can recite the *Blow, Boys, Blow.*'"

So much for my place in life, my destiny, he thought, and sank far enough to find a small ledge upon which he precariously placed his rump. Much better than laying upon the damp earth.

Not sure of how much time had expired, nor if he slept. With the blackness cloaking his space, he thought that he probably did sleep. Upon listening intently to something… panting… breathing. Not him. Fearing the worst, perhaps some wild animal to use him for its' next meal, he spoke, "Man or beast?"

Hearing a gentle snicker, then a sweetly feminine voice, "Open your eyes, Sir. I see you are in a great deal of trouble. Master Featherstone has his men bring his victims for safekeeping to this place until they are ready to be put out to parts unknown to me."

Opening his eyes wide, they quickly adjusted to the small candle held by a petite hand, then glanced upward into a young face featuring dark eyes and an abundance of long black tresses held back with a blue band. "My name is Pakuma. I will take you to safety. Can you walk?"

Looking down, Ryan said, "We'll soon see. Help me to stand." Once upright, he tested his leg strength with a couple slight bounces; then nodding, he said, "Please, untie my hands and let's get out of here. No telling when that bunch will be back to get me. I wish they'd left my boots and belt. I feel naked without them." He smiled.

Following the girl as quietly as he could, he heard himself grunt and moan with the aches and pains of the misuse of his body. "Try to keep silent, sir."

35

Whispering toward the back of her head, "I'll do my best, and you can call me Ryan."

Silently they tread through the meandering tunnels. Ryan had to completely trust this new friend, because alone he'd be totally lost. The way she took him was confusing:... first one way and then another, seemingly without any direction. She'd stop periodically and light a fresh candle from the stub of the previous one. As it was, the candles were small to begin with and burned up rather quickly, but he was content with her evident knowledge of the dark spaces.

Finally, after what seemed like a mile, the girl stopped and motioned for Ryan to remain silent, and for him to stay back until she could ascertain the safety of their exit. Walking quietly outward through a thicket of shrubs, Pakuma emerged to complete tranquility. No other soul anywhere near, nor, for that matter was there any threat from wild animals. Only the evening birds to be heard. She knew the sounds were truly of birds and not imitations. Stepping back, she whispered for Ryan to follow her out of hiding and into a wide field of high grasses. "Stay behind me. Step in my steps so there will appear to be only one travelling. We want to make finding you as difficult as possible. And, be quiet. Say nothing, make no sound. Just stay close and use my steps; then, if you can, sweep up as much of the trodden grass as you can to cover our way."

Ryan nodded in total understanding. He estimated they walked the equivalent of five or six miles before Pakuma stopped. She turned, took his hand, and pulled him down beside her in a stream bed. "Drink now. We have a little while yet before we come to my home. How are your feet? Let me look."

Sitting on a large smooth boulder, slaking his thirst, he felt her fingers pressing upon the soles of his feet. The ministrations were painful, but he could tell she was making an estimate of how much attention the feet would need before they'd become infected and need more than she could provide.

"How much further?"

"Very close now. This is where my people get water." Pakuma replied. "We are very few now. The boss took most of our village, even some of the young girls and boys. There are only two old ones and five younger than me now left. Our little ones died when their mothers were taken. We try to stay hidden, and we move often." Pakuma paused only long enough to gather her thoughts. "You see, our land here held many different tribes. The Miwok, of which I am one of few left, are not the only tribe to be killed off. We were slain like vermin by the influx of men of all races who invaded here. We were slaughtered because the invaders feared they could not trust us."

"Why do you help me? Am I not also of those who killed and stole your people?"

"No, you were to be used as we have been. I saw my chance to save you from them. This gives us some little victory over them and their evil ways. Now, come let us finish our journey. We are nearly home."

. . .

The clearing was a total surprise to Ryan. He and Pakuma were stepping through heavy woods without any indication of a settlement, and suddenly they were in the middle of four structures built entirely of limbs and leaves. The vestiges of a fire could be imagined if one peered closely, and there was not a sound or soul anywhere. "Uncle. You are safe. I have brought one to be saved."

Moving into view came an old man, withered and wiry with long grey hair. He was overdressed by the fact that he wore at least three shirts and enough trousers as to appear to be padded. Coming out from behind him was a woman holding the hands of two younger boys. Three young women also stepped forward to stand silently and emotionless.

"This is Ryan. He was taken from a ship by those working for Boss. I thought it would be good to save him. He may be able to help us too."

"That is good, Pakuma. You have done well. He is welcome here. But how do you propose to dress him for warmth.?The weather is soon to turn cold and he has not enough to wear."

"Since he is now with us and can do the work, I will have the time to make for him what he needs for now. He will bring the food. I will make the garments and moccasins." Smiling, she looked directly at Ryan. "You will bring the deer and puma and bear, Ryan."

Shaking his head, Ryan quickly tried to make them understand that not only did he have no protection for his feet, but he did not have a gun. If by some miracle he did have a gun, he had no ammunition. "I wish I could hunt for your family, Pakuma, but I have nothing with which to go hunting. The only gift I am able to provide is trapping. I am well able to fashion secure traps and I will provide all the furs you can have need of as well as the meat of that which is caught."

Nodding and smiling, the old man stepped close and said, "You will be taught. You are intelligent in your eyes. You are very strong and silent. You will do well here and will learn quickly." Turning to Pakuma, he said, "We must feed before night. Quickly now, prepare."

The old woman led Ryan into a small shelter and bade him sit while she placed sections of food onto a broad leaf. Ryan had no idea what the repast consisted of, but it mattered not. He ate without so much as a sidewise glance. His new friends smiled and nodded as he devoured it all. Ryan thought to himself, *I'll find out soon enough what I've just eaten; now all that matters is that it's food!*

Pakuma told Ryan to lie down if he thought he could sleep, but Ryan shook his head and said, "I need to relieve my body. Where should I go?"

She slipped out of the shelter and pointed to a thicket of shrubs, saying, "Step through and to the west side; the other way is used now. You must use the west. Understand?"

Ryan smiled and nodded, then walked quietly toward where she'd indicated.

He soon returned to the shelter and lay down where he'd been seated for the meal. Within a very short time he was snuffling softly and Pakuma slipped the fur side of a hide across his body. He never moved.

• • •

For the next several months, the little band moved three times. Each time they found themselves farther from the cave where Ryan had been kept. Each previous camp site was obliterated so thoroughly no one of ordinary intelligence would ever consider anyone had made that place their home. Ryan was an apt pupil to every instruction by old Sewatee. He learned the chipping of obsidian into arrowheads, the choosing of limbs to fashion into strong bows and the fine sinews for bow strings, and the art of soundless movement. Running silently without cracking a twig became easy. Tempering his breathing to his beating heart in order to run mile upon mile with little effort. Tracking whatever animals in the vicinity of where the little tribe found themselves became second nature. Ryan recalled having been told that he must always be mindful of his thought processes. He did. He learned. He expanded his life by leaps and bounds.

Pakuma and Wauna worked diligently to stitch together the hides and furs for clothing and coverings for the cold months ahead. The boys, young Oya and Tukuli, were proficient at cleaning fish, as well as gutting and skinning smaller game like squirrels and rabbits. The three girls—Huata, Kamata, and Sanuye—were kept busy at cooking, tending the fire pit and keeping the tightly-woven baskets filled with water. They gathered every acorn that could be found and felt very fortunate to come upon a large buckeye tree. The preparation of both nuts was laborious but well worth the effort since they provided thickening to the stews as well as being utilized as a type of bread. They gathered native fruits and berries at every propitious moment and prepared them for drying and stringing for storage. Ever diligent and industrious, the dedicated group made provision for the onset of winter.

While out scouting for food one early morning, Ryan came upon a crevice into which he'd seen a rabbit disappear. Slipping silently toward the spot, he was pleasantly surprised to find a narrow, hidden opening to a small shallow cave. Just a convenient size to house his tribe of nine to be sheltered from the winter elements. Forgetting about the rabbit, he slipped around the perimeter of the mounds of earth to see how well it was protected from intruders approaching from any direction. Satisfying himself that the hidden opening was indeed the only way in, he checked the lay of the land from all angles in order to be able to lead his family to this place as soon as possible. He knew Sewatee and Wauna would be happy to have such protection, especially for the younger ones, during the coming winter months.

Upon his return to their camp he was greeted by Pakuma, who took the pack of furs from his back while the boys began cleaning the fish Ryan had brought.

That night at supper, Ryan explained to them about the small cavity he'd found near the base of the mountains. Sewatee agreed that he would go and inspect the site with Ryan to see as to its feasibility.

Chapter V

S tanding with Ryan inside the cave, the old man nodded. With silence and a soft smile, the two returned to their present camp. Sewatee told the family that it would be best for them to arrange to transfer there at the earliest possible time.

During the move, Ryan became aware that they had more than enough furs for the family's needs, so he decided to take the remainder down into the settlement of Coloma to barter for foods and other items he thought his family would appreciate having.

It had been many, many moons since he'd gone missing from Captain Witherspoon in San Francisco. However, knowing that where he was going might be near to where the boss would have his hirelings ever on the lookout for their escaped prisoner, Ryan hoped by the fact that he now sported a long beard and long hair, dressed in buckskins and moccasins with a bearskin cape and hat, he'd never be recognized.

Pakuma and Wauna helped get the furs stacked and packed so Ryan could easily lift the bundle atop his shoulders and still carry his bow and arrows. Ryan bade them all goodbye and told them he felt he'd be back within two weeks at most.

. . .

Entering the bustling settlement of Coloma, his presence never elicited a raised brow. He fit in with the busy goings on, as did the other odd-humans. He quickly found the trading post and headed there.

After having secured the needed supplies as well as a few coins, he began considering whether or not to head back into the wilderness or utilize some of his money for a hearty meal. He opted for a warm meal to fill his belly. He'd plan to bed down on the trail once he headed back toward the mountains.

Chapter VI

While seated at a community table in a small kitchen, he kept his head down but his ears up. How grateful he was for his thought processes. He found himself listening to several men speaking of a certain Captain Sutter who had evidently bought a large acreage on the Sacramento River for his fort and some on the American River in order to build and erect a mill which would saw timber into building wood. The man had foresight enough to know this area of God's earth was quickly being settled by people of all sects and economic statuses. They would ultimately have need of building materials. After all, the very *Narcissus* had sailed from New York Port to San Francisco Port with as much needed wood and building supplies as could be stowed. It stood to reason then that a mill of that sort would certainly be welcome and would provide lumber at a greatly decreased cost.

He also overheard that this Captain Sutter was hiring hale and hearty men who could actually build the mill and excavate the millrace from the river. As Ryan was picking up his empty platter and stein, he quickly spoke to the most informative man who was seated across the table.

"Sir, please excuse my interruption, but would you be willing to provide to me the whereabouts of the place of this hiring activity? I believe I could be of some benefit in that endeavor."

"And who would you be, son?"

"I'm just a trapper, sir, making my way with the wilds and wonders of this land. You can call me Trenton, sir, if it pleases you."

"Well, I must say you've got quite a silver tongue. You come from educated stock?"

Smiling, Ryan replied, "Afraid not, sir. I simply have an ear for speech, and enjoy the art of being as proper as I can."

All the men laughed and slapped the top of the long table, causing dishes to rattle slightly. "I must say, young Trenton, you're an entertainment as well." Becoming serious, the man continued, "I figure you'll be well worth your hire. Will you be taking your morning meal here?"

"I had not planned on it, sir, but If you believe it would be to my advantage to do so, then I shall."

"Be here on the morrow as soon as you spy the smoke from the kitchen chimneys."

"I look forward to it, sir." And bending slightly from his waist, seeking all the eyes of those at the table, Ryan turned and silently left the building.

• • •

Taking in a lungful of cooling night air, he contained his ebullience. Turning eastward out of the settlement, he made his way along the river until he found the place where he'd bed down for the night. He dreamed of running through a leafless forest, trailing an unseen animal of magnificent proportions, one he must capture if for no other reason than its rarity.

Well before sunrise, he awoke to an unexpected sound. Maintaining his silence and hidden position, he strained to determine, if possible, exactly what it was and where it was. He became aware of nearby breathing. *Pakuma!* "Man or beast?" he spoke quietly.

"Ah, Ryan, you knew it was me. You are too keen. It is as if you were born Indian," she replied.

"Why are you here? Is anything wrong?"

"Everything is alright. Just Old Sewatee sent me to see if you could use me in some way. He says he knows you will be long here, and thought you might need something," she said.

"Do you have all you will need for the winter? Furs and foods?"

"Yes. With all we have gathered and what you and Sewatee brought in, we are well prepared. Wauna and the young ones will do well now that we have the new place high in the mountains. We are safe there until your return."

"I'm happy you have come, Pakuma. I have been blessed by trading the furs for our needed supplies. After you rest a while, I will pack them for your return home."

"So soon? You will not need me for even a few days? Can I not be of some help to you? What do you plan to do while you stay in the white man's village?"

"I plan to help build a fixture near the river that will cut timber into lumber for the construction of other buildings. I will be able to provide more for our family in just a few short months. By spring, I should be finished and can return to get us moved. Maybe it can be for the last time. I can set you up in a more comfortable abode."

"Oh, Ryan. I fear we are not made for such a dwelling. We are people of the land and won't know how to be happy trying to live any other way than what we know."

"Alright, Pakuma. Come, lie down and rest. We'll talk more of this later. I must rise early to get you prepared to return because I will leave to meet a man to begin my work here. I would like you to stay, but you cannot. You must return home to care for them until I return to you by spring. Now, come and sleep. Lie here next to me." Ryan settled Pakuma by his side and laid the furs over her body. She turned with a slight huff, but was soon breathing softly. He smiled and slept.

•   •   •

Striding into the kitchen, Ryan was glad he'd gotten to the meeting place before the other gentleman he was to meet. He ordered breakfast and was nearly finished when the man came in. He smiled at Ryan and spoke, "A hearty good morning to you, Mr. Trenton. I'm happy to see you so prompt. That says a great deal of your character." Continuing, he said, "Let me get my breakfast ordered then I'll sit down and we can talk in peace."

He walked to the opening in back and loudly shouted out his order of steak and potatoes with biscuits and gravy and a potful of coffee. Turning, he came back and slid onto the long bench across from Ryan. He reached his hand across the span and Ryan laid his own into it. The men shook hands, and then the businessman continued, "My name is James Marshall, Trenton, and I'm the boss for Captain Sutter. It's in my hands to get his orders carried out as quickly and as inexpensively as is possible. He does not want me to skimp on the materials used in the buildings, but he does want me to hire on people that will do a full day's work for a full day's wage. If you earn your wage I will pay you well. Thus far we have hired on a number of natives, some Mexicans, and even a couple of Mormon soldiers left over from the war. Four Russians had been here but they left before we could get all the wood offloaded from the *Narcissus* and brought to the site here."

He stopped speaking and began to dig into his breakfast.

"Mr. Marshall, sir, I'll give you and your boss my very best effort. I'm fairly strong and I believe I will be of some good benefit to your endeavor."

"I believe so too, Trenton. Here, have another cup of this coffee." And he reached over and filled the empty cup next to Ryan's elbow.

• • •

Before nightfall Ryan had been apprised of the entire project and, because of his excellent thought processes, was even able to suggest alternatives to lighten the labor and to save funds. James considered that he'd certainly made an excellent move in hiring on this young man. He was anxious to have him meet Captain Sutter at first opportunity.

Within four weeks the skeleton of the mill was taking shape and the paddle wheel was ready to accept the axel. The laborers had dug a fair-sized millrace which swung in a slight arc from the American River. It was planned, once the ditch was deep and wide enough, to suspend the paddle wheel from the axel, which would extend from the gears inside the mill.

Upon measuring and re-measuring the width and depth of the wheel, Marshall felt the ditch was sufficient. Ryan was down in the ditch with two other men as the wheel was slowly lowered to them. As the wheel was held perpendicular and lifted to fit onto the axel, it soon became evident that the ditch needed to be at least another three feet deeper. Ryan told his foreman that there needed to be enough depth of water to come up to at least two thirds of the lower half of the wheel in order for there to be enough water-thrust to give the wheel forceful turning. He told him the water force must be extremely strong to run the gears fast enough for the saws to cut the timber.

That evening at supper, Ryan explained to Mr. Marshall that instead of having the men dig and cast out shovelfuls of dirt up onto the banks, that they ought to build barriers to hold the water back at the junctions where the ditch met the river both at the entrance and at the exit. Then every evening just at quitting time, they could open the slue and allow the river to rush through, thereby carrying the loosened dirt away in the flow and on down river. Not only would this action expedite the deepening of the ditch, it would be less laborious on the men doing the digging.

The suggestion was well received by Marshall and the actions were taken. Just a few days later, they were ready to try the lowering of the wheel again. Ryan was standing in chest-deep water with James as three other workers jimmied the wheel over the edge of the building and slowly lowered it down. The flow of the water made it difficult for the two men to settle the hub onto the axel so the wheel was lifted back up. It was decided that the upper junction would be closed off and the lower one left open to drain the water long enough for them to get the wheel set.

As Ryan and James began pushing their way up the ditch, heading for the upper closure, they began to notice the sparkle of millions of gold flakes swirling around their bodies. "My God, Trenton. Do you suppose this is what it looks like?"

"Better not say anything, Mr. Marshall. But I do believe it is what we think it is. We'd better close off the flow and get to Captain Sutter as fast as we can."

"What ought I to do about the laborers?"

"Tell them to take the rest of the week off and be back on Monday. Tell them we've got to let the ditch drain for the time being. We need to get out of here and head to the Captain." They closed off the millrace and opened the lower tailrace to allow the water to flow out. As the water subsided, they saw nuggets of gold literally piled and scattered among the washed stone. They gathered up what could be easily reached and left as soon as possible for Captain Sutter's home, which was about forty miles up on the Sacramento River.

Upon arriving at Sutter's home in a pouring, cold rain, the men were welcomed and brought in to dry off. He had hot coffee braced with brandy for a tad of comfort for them and then settled to inspect the nuggets. "Gentlemen, I realize this is gold, but there is probably not enough to mess with. I'd much prefer to go on with the plans to finish the saw mill. I believe this will be more beneficial to me than anything else. See to it that no one else knows of your discovery, alright?"

"Yes sir. This is your call. We'll keep it quiet, and go on as planned."

"How is the construction going?"

"We were ready hang the wheel onto the axel. We'll get that done probably on Monday, and then can proceed to finishing the gears and laying in the saws and belts. It should be up and running within a week if all goes as planned," said Marshall.

"Wonderful. I'll make a trip down as soon as this weather tempers somewhat." Rising to go to the open hall, he said, "Hattie, come please." In very short order a rotund Mexican girl showed at the door. "Sir?"

"Get the room ready for my two guests, please."

"Oh, no sir, Captain. We cannot stay. We must return to Coloma and get all prepared for the men to begin early on Monday. We need to get that wheel set as soon as possible so we can let the water back in the ditch. Until the water is flowing again, there's a chance someone will spy some of the gold that may be exposed."

"You headed back tonight? In this weather?"

"Yes, sir, we must." Both men shook hands with Sutter and left immediately. Heads down in the driving rain, the men made a miserable trip back to the little settlement of Coloma.

Saturday morning when they arrived at the mill site, there were several men digging in the tailrace for the nuggets. "Too late!" both Ryan and Marshall spoke together.

Every man that had been hired on by Marshall left for panning. The hordes of people plowed up and down the American River elbowing for room. Stakes were made and gold was found. James Marshall, disheartened, fled the area. Ryan headed to his home and family. And the little settlement of Coloma burst at the seams. Soon a land office was set up by the government, as well as a surveying team. A bank was established by a Mr. Brannon. Attorneys settled in. Saloons sprouted up. Hotels and houses were soon built. A community church was established. And Ryan's little family lived in secluded peace.

The long winter passed and the landscape greened up once more. Trees budded out and birds hatched new clutches of babies. Mother rabbits lined their earthen nests with their softest fur; the young kits began to venture forth. Bears awoke from sleep and foraged in the icy streams for their sustenance as Ryan and his family began a new round of hunting-gathering. The comfort of their cave home was truly the best place they'd ever been. The location was ideal in that it not only provided security, but also convenience. The temperature remained constant near the rear of the cave when it was closed off with stitched hides hung like curtains across the narrow adit.

Even when they had small fires within the cave, the resultant smoke never became overpowering, nor choking. Ryan suspected that, even though no rain ever came into their dwelling, there must be some small aperture somewhere which prompted the rising smoke to dissipate into the outside. He'd been all over and around the cave but had never seen nor suspected where the release actually was. Being thankful for small favors, he never broached the subject with any of his family.

Chapter VII

The spring rains came and the water ran in rivulets along the front of the place. The little family remained dry and secure behind the curtain. Periodically Pakuma would fasten back the drape to allow fresh air to enter and sweeten their home.

Ryan was out tending to his snares and traps, meanwhile hunting anything that he happened upon. Drenched to his bones, he was grateful for the cleansing of his buckskins and body. Barely chilled by the downpour, he pressed on happily with his burdens. Pakuma was standing just outside the entrance watching for Ryan, when suddenly the children, followed by Wauna and Sewatee, ran out of the cave, nearly knocking Pakuma to the ground. "What is the matter?" she begged. She saw the fear in the eyes of the children.

They gathered near her and pointed back into the cave. "What? Sewatee, tell me!"

"The top has fallen in on everything. It is filling up the cave. There is even a small tree in the sleeping place. It will be some time before we'll be able to see exactly what did happen."

Ryan heard the thunderous sound from the collapse and began to run, his game and hides bouncing across his shoulders and he sped toward home. At last he was at the rock steps leading up to his home.

Looking up, he saw his family gathered in a knot in the pouring rain. Breathing a prayer of thanks that they all seemed to be well, he quickly arrived to where they were waiting for him. "What happened, Sewatee?"

"The top of our home has collapsed from all the rain and now rests inside. I think it has completed its venture by now. We'll try to get in and see what damage has been done."

Shrugging his shoulders toward the young boys, Ryan said, "Yes. Here, Tukule and Oya, take the game and begin cleaning it for our meal. You girls, quickly now.... Spread the curtain from the opening over some bent limbs to provide shelter. Plait a lean-to with leaves and sticks for our fire pit. Our supply of firewood was kept high enough. Hopefully, it will not have been affected by the collapse. Pakuma and Wauna, I will bring out the pot. It might not even need to be cleaned. You get the cooking begun as soon as the girls have the fire pit ready. Come, Sewatee, let us see to the damage."

None of the family was ever aware of just when Ryan became chief, but that event simply evolved. He took the reins without any forethought or reservations. As the men entered the cave, they were greeted with a raft of mud and roots and small plants and trees. Looking skyward they witnessed the rain coming down with nothing to preclude its descent. "No need to try to work in this place right now. We must hold off until the rain stops. Meantime, let us help outside to set up some shelter in which to eat and sleep this night."

Working diligently the family was able to, despite being still soaked to their skin, form an area beneath cover to build a fire, which they added to as the wood dried and burned higher. The boys spitted the small game over the fire and kept it turned to cook through. Wauna boiled dried knobs of ground acorns and added to it wild onions and the seeds of dried beans gathered from last summer's crop. As soon as the game was cooked through, it was added to the pot and made a savory stew. Pakuma threw in a small amount of the salt she'd brought back from Coloma when she had visited with Ryan earlier.

Sitting near the fire, the group had begun to dry somewhat, and having enveloped their surroundings with branches thick with leaves, they were almost free from the falling rain. In fact, Oya left the fire to relieve himself and upon his return announced, "The rain has stopped and the sky is clearing; I can see the moon through the scudding clouds!"

"Good. First order of the day: After breakfast we begin to clear the cave enough to see if we can stay, or if we will need to move."

"I want to stay here, Ryan. It has truly become a home to me. One to which you always will return." Pakuma spoke her heart.

Listening to Pakuma's remarks to Ryan, Sewatee and Wauna glanced at each other as they understood Pakuma desired to be a wife to Ryan. Sewatee knew that Ryan had never considered such a relationship with Pakuma. He saw month after month the hopes of Pakuma stepped upon by the handsome Ryan. Sewatee decided he must speak to Ryan as soon as possible about this situation. They would be working closely together on clearing the cave. He'd hope to use that time to speak.

• • •

"Looks like if we can get the larger sections of wood out in one piece, we may be able to use them to shore up a new roof. At least until we can determine that we want to stay here." Ryan and Sewatee labored all morning without a break. Finally, Pakuma came bearing water and food. The men stopped long enough to sit and discuss with Pakuma their findings.

Ryan spoke, "It appears that only a small section of the top gave way. Two pines caved through without breaking. If we can dig out the rest of the mud and roots, I think I can use the trees to hold a woven platform even with the earth up top to install a small pipe to allow the smoke to escape. I can place layers of straw and earth deep enough for the grass to take root and cover us once more. Once that's done, we can drive strong wooden stakes into the top of the cave across enough places until it will form a sturdy ceiling. After some time, I think we'd be able to remove the upright pines, unless they become useful to hang stuff on." Then he continued, "We found the fissure where the smoke had been filtering out before the collapse, and that's where the break started. I don't believe it will take too much for us to make it livable again. If you trust me to do it."

"Oh yes, Ryan, we trust you. We know you are capable and want to provide for your family. We all will help. You only need to tell us what you want done." They all nodded and smiled. Pakuma could "see" herself and Ryan raising their children here.

Climbing atop the debris piled inside the cave, Ryan drove spiked limbs into the upper walls of the cave from one side into the other. Placing the logs closely together, he soon had a fairly tight ceiling beneath which he jammed the two pines upright to secure everything. The girls were set to placing boughs over the ceiling around a pipe that Ryan had made from a cow horn. They added layer upon layer of muddy earth, and then finished it off with plugs of tall grass. One would never even know there was a "horn chimney" there.

Digging away the mud inside took three days of constant work. The men used the mud to form a ridge around the narrow opening to direct rainwater away from the entrance. One needed to step up over the barrier, but they felt it also would help keep the snows from blowing in. Wauna had sewn a large, heavy fur curtain that had been very good in keeping warmth in and cold out. Now that the weather had tempered, the curtain had been removed and was serving as the roof of their lean-to home for the time being.

Pakuma was bringing in armloads of straw to lay on the cave floor to help soak up as much of the moisture as possible, as well as to mix with the dampness and give more comfort underfoot. Wauna was sweeping down the walls with a bundle of fine branches tied together when Ryan happened to look toward the back. "Wauna, sweep back here for me. This is a new part of the cave we did not have before the collapse. We never knew this was here. We've got enough room now to where we can expand and have more space. Come see, Sewatee, Pakuma." Ryan lifted the lantern so the new area could be explored.

Ryan's eyes adjusted to the dim interior, and there he saw three wide veins of gold running like fire along the undulating walls. He nearly dropped the lantern. The four stood silently. Ryan's thought processes were racing at this find. "Well, friends, it looks as though we've really struck gold. We must not say anything to anyone outside this family or we will lose our home here. Let us continue to clean and prepare this place for ourselves. We will talk about this later on. Right now we've got work to do." *Oh Lord, is this to be my destiny? Am I to place my future here with Pakuma and this family?*

They helped Ryan get packed for his trip down to Coloma and the trading post. There were enough beaver furs alone to buy all the supplies they needed. He bade them goodbye and told them he'd be home within ten days.

Once in Coloma, Ryan took his furs to Mister Claymore at the trading post. Since the influx of so many more people to Coloma, the return on his furs had greatly risen, and he decided to stay at the hotel, pay for a bath, and have a filling meal before seeing the land officer.

Next morning Ryan ventured into the land office. A Mister Landry had recently become a fixture there, brought by the presence of so many panhandlers needing to file for stakes. Ryan wanted to secure the cave while he had the opportunity. He stomped the dust from his newly-purchased boots and entered the office. A bespectacled, baldheaded gentleman was seated at a large table which was literally piled with papers left and right with two inkwells centered between. He was busily scribbling across one sheet when he looked up at Ryan's entrance. "Morning sir, what can I do for you?" he asked.

"Morning. My name is Trenton and I'd like to get my section of the world secured by title at your convenience."

"Sit down, please. I'll be with you in just a few minutes. I must attend to this matter while it's fresh on my mind." He motioned for Ryan to take a chair facing his desk. He continued to write for another five minutes or so, then he laid the pen down and sat back, sliding the paper atop the pile on the right end of the table. He stood, leaned forward with hand extended, and said, "I'm Carl Landry at your service. Now how may I help you, Trenton?"

"I make my home at the base of the Sierra Nevada in a small cave. I have a family of eight souls that rely on me for their care. You see, sir, they are displaced Miwok Indians, what's left of an entire tribe. Four girls, two boys, and an old woman and man."

Nodding, Mr. Landry asked, "Not that it's any of my business, Trenton, but exactly how did you become caretaker of a bunch of displaced Indians?"

Ryan held his breath long enough to maintain his temper, then said, "Sir, I perceive you hold some animosity toward the indigents of this land. Is that correct?"

"By no means. I apologize for giving that impression. My choice of words was unfortunate, but I am curious about your situation. Especially since the majority of clients entering these doors seek to secure a stake for panning for the golden goddess that roams through these lands at this present time. I beg your indulgence to my query, sir."

"The answer to your question is simple. I was kidnapped from a trader ship moored in San Francisco Bay two years back. The miscreants had me hog-tied awaiting orders, when a young Miwok girl rescued me. You see, these same men had decimated their village, killing all except those taken as slaves. The few left had been away from the village at the time doing other chores, only to return to find the carnage of those decapitated or cut to pieces. After burying the remains, they fled to a life on the run, moving from one camp site to another every few weeks. Pakuma—my rescuer—happened to be in the process of searching for a new campsite when she found the hidden back end of the cave. Exploring it for possible use by her family, she found where the men had been holding those they kidnapped. She led several away to safety because she was trying to interfere with their nefarious business. I just happened to be found by her. She trusted me for some reason and took me to their camp. The family taught me to live as an Indian. They cared for and fed me. I, in return, care for and feed them. Does this help your understanding of my situation?"

"Indeed, sir. And I commend you on your honesty and uprightness in dealing with those of such unfortunate circumstances. The natives of this land have surely been dealt a devilish blow by the invaders. But, now! Down to the business for which you came." Reaching to a fresh stack of papers, Mister Landry wrote across the top of two sheets the date and place of this initial meeting for an explanation of its purpose.

"You will need to provide a veritable description of where this property is located for the charts-men to locate it, and within a few days, or weeks at the most, they will attend to this business for you, and if this particular section has not been filed on previously, then it shall certainly be granted to you. So, friend, come now and give me your most detailed description of the whereabouts of this mountain cave of yours."

· · ·

Ryan arrived back home before the eighth day had passed. Pakuma was the first one to see Ryan coming up the steep incline toward the adit to their home. Running down the incline to meet him, she skidded to a stop directly in front of Ryan, and with no prelude or pretense, reached up to hug him close. Taken somewhat aback, Ryan stood with arms akimbo, as Pakuma stretched upward to kiss his lips. As their lips touched, he slipped his arms around her and held her just long enough to realize exactly what affect this contact between them elicited. Drawing back, Ryan put her away from him. "Pakuma, that's quite a homecoming welcome." He hoped his words helped to cool her ardor. He could not afford to allow her to pursue this path. He knew that he had plans to leave this family one day, and so was determined to leave with as little notice as possible. He'd see to it that they were settled and situated in such a way as to be self-sufficient and secure. By no stretch of his imagination could Ryan see himself with this clan of people as his true destiny.

"We are so happy to have you home again. Much has been done inside the cave since you left. We have even curtained off some sections for more privacy. Since the collapse opened up more of the cave, we now have the room. Wauna thought you may want your own space away from Sewatee and Oya and Tukuli. Come now and see."

Ryan took a deep breath and thought, *This is going to be more complicated than I ever considered. I'll worry about it later.* "Alright, Pakuma, show me what you all have done."

•   •   •

That evening after the family had eaten and had begun to drowse, Sewatee asked, "Tell us what you found out in Coloma about our home, Ryan."

"The land office will send a team of men to come here and help me stake out the place—that is, if it doesn't already belong to someone else. If this property is already staked out, then we will need to leave. As far as I can see, though, no one has ever been near this place; so, if it is free, we will become the owners of it. I've already drawn a semblance of the area to include the land all the way around the hill and downward to the base toward the river. Now all we have to do is wait."

"Will the men be curious to see our home? Won't we need to welcome them and offer them food while they labor here?" asked Wauna.

Sitting silently for a few moments, Ryan began to see the meaning behind what Wauna had just said. "Yes!" he replied. "You are right. We must do something to cover the veins of gold on the walls. Only how will we be able to do that so it appears natural?"

Smiling, Wauna spoke, "You just leave it to Pakuma and me. We know exactly what to do. It may take us two or three days, but you have no fear. You will never know where the gold is once we get through."

"I trust you both. Do you need anything from me to help in your plans?"

"As you go about your hunting and checking the traps, just look for pine hearts. Bring any you find. It will help save the candles."

Ryan had no idea exactly what Wauna meant, but he'd do his best to bring as much of the sappy wood as he could cut and drag home.

• • •

Early one glorious morning about six weeks after his visit to the land office, two men stopped at the base of the rock stairs and called up to the opening they could barely see. The area, they felt sure, was the right place, judging by the drawing that Ryan had made to identify the land for their arrival.

Young Tukuli ran to the front of the cave and motioned for the men to come on up. He ran back inside to tell Wauna that the men were on their way. Sewatee was out fishing, Ryan was away checking his traps, and Pakuma was out with the younger girls picking berries and gathering acorns and horse chestnuts. Wauna and the two young boys were the only ones at the place.

Wauna met the men at the entrance and invited them in for a rest and food before they were to begin their work.

"Say, this is sure okay. Nice and dry and cozy. How long you been here?" asked the taller of the men.

"Take a seat, sir. My name is Wauna and these are my grandsons, Oya and Tukuli. Let me give you some water, or something to eat. There is deer stew still on the fire. It's very good and filling. You will need something to hold you while you do your work."

"You here all by yourself?" asked the taller one.

"No. My two grandsons are here, as you can see. If you do not want water or food, then you must go and get your job done. My son will want to see you are busy when he returns. I know he has already paid to have you do this. You do not want to be sitting doing nothing should he return soon."

"Oh yeah? Where is he now? Is he sure to be back soon?" asked the taller one. The shorter man was walking around the cave touching things and looking at everything, glancing up at the walls and ceiling.

"You will leave now since you do not want to rest." Wauna went to the cave opening as Oya and Tukuli stood at the back holding spears. The men began to realize they would need to get out. They could not take a chance on riling the boys. The men, Joseph and Henry, had pistols, but they weren't foolish enough to think they'd harm the old woman and boys just for fun. They headed to the front of the cave as Ryan stood there watching them. "You two having some difficulty getting started this morning?"

"No sir. We were just admiring your home. We'll begin our mapping now. Looks like you and your family will have a nice place here bein' as how it's never been spoken for."

"As soon as I check out the place, I'll join you men to make sure you get everything I want on that map. I want everything I paid for. You understand? I have already cut over fifty tall stakes that I want you to use. I'll be down to help you in a few minutes." Ryan quickly took Wauna by the arm and led her back into the cave. "What did they do? Do you think they suspect anything?"

"All is well. They just wanted to make me and the boys feel they were in charge. Wanted to make me feel afraid. They looked all around but never even made any kind of motion that they thought this was anything but a plain cave."

"Good. I'll get out there and see that they get this done right."

It took several hours for Joseph and Henry to complete the survey to Ryan's specifications. As each section was assured, Ryan drove the long stakes down into the earth and then pulled a red-dyed strip of sinew into the slit ends of each one. "Gentlemen, I am satisfied that you've completed your job here. I'll be checking back with Mr. Landry in a few days to give him my appreciation of your work." Extending his hand, Ryan bade the men, "Have a pleasant trip back to Coloma, and a safe one."

He stood silently to watch the two descend the mountain and did not move until they were well out of sight. Finally, Wauna sent Pakuma to fetch him for the evening meal. "Come, Ryan, you must eat now. We have prepared your meal. There is fresh fish Sewatee caught today."

Coming into the well-lit interior, Ryan sat in his usual spot to begin the meal. After a few minutes, he looked toward the rear of the place and asked how they were able to cover the large veins of gold. Smiling broadly, Wauna spoke, "You brought us plenty of pine hearts. Oya and

Tukuli lit them for Pakuma and me to wave them across the walls and the smoke covered the places in thick soot. Very good for cover, and very good for hiding at night. Many times we were not found because we rubbed our clothes, as well as our skin, with the black. It is a gift from the Great Spirit."

"Yes, Wauna, a great gift from the Great Spirit. And He has given us this cave as well as the gold for us to make our security in the white man's world that has come into the Miwok lands. The stranger is now boss in your land and because this is so, we must begin to prepare you to live in their world, to learn their ways, at least enough to be able to raise the girls and boys to make their way in it. The gold will help us to do that. Right now, we need to take our rest and talk more of this tomorrow."

That night Pekuna thought long and hard about what Ryan had said. She wondered where her place would be... *With Ryan?* That's what her deepest desire was—to be with Ryan. She began to speak to the Great Spirit about her desire. Soon, her thoughts morphed into pleasant dreams.

Chapter VIII

T he family only uncovered a small section of the vein at a time, digging and loosening the pliable metal. They kept it secreted within the water skins, as well as within patches sewn onto the curtains within the cave. Ryan took the larger pieces and deliberately broke them up into small chunks in order that the blower would not suspect he'd found it in such large amounts. With strangers awash in Coloma, ever on the lookout for the advantage to take over a stake, murder was not beneath them. Ryan did not want to expose his family to the greed of others. Consequently he needed to be extra vigilant when bringing in his gold for the blowers to weigh.

On his initial foray into Coloma with a small amount of gold hidden upon himself, he headed directly to the one man—at this point in time— whom he felt he could trust: Carl Landry of the land office. Entering the musty room, Ryan spoke, "Good morning, Carl. Glad to see you are still among the settlers of Coloma."

Standing, Carl greeted his acquaintance with an outstretched hand. "Yes, Mr. Trenton! How pleasant to greet you once again." Sitting and indicating a facing chair to Ryan, he asked, "What may I do for you today?"

"The charts-men you recommended for my claim were excellent. I am very pleased with the job they did. I helped, in that I drove the marked stakes everywhere they indicated, and I believe I possibly have more land than I paid for. Could you check the files and give a final determination as to whether I do owe more?"

"By all means, Mister Trenton, by all means." Rising from his desk chair and reaching a large chest with many shallow drawers, he withdrew a detailed map of the area of Ryan's claim. Laying the sheet atop the table, he turned to motion for Ryan to join him in the perusal of the chart. "This line here…" his finger pointing to a blue inked line, "shows where you originally thought you'd like to claim. It includes all of the outlying areas surrounding the cave in which you abide. It runs across this small stream and down the mountain to include the wide ascending pathway upward." Glancing at Ryan, he said, "You paid for everything within that blue area. I see here by the marks made by the Henry and Joe that you desire the addition of a few more yards here, which takes in more of the runoff into the stream where you obtain water. This would be the only part you might owe anything on. Did the men mention that you might owe them?"

"No, sir, they did not, but I feel I must indeed give them something more for their trouble, even though I did help in the driving of the stakes."

"Well, I feel sure they are satisfied or they would have mentioned it. However, if you feel so inclined, I will certainly contact the men and speak with them concerning your feelings. But, come now, it's near dinnertime and I'm starving. Will you join me for one of the splendid meals in the newest hotel in Coloma? I promise you won't be disappointed."

"Wonderful! I'd be happy to. And, I'd like to speak with you about another of my concerns I want to settle while here on this trip into civilization."

Laughing, the men left the land office and headed down the boardwalk toward a new two-story building.

Ryan's mind was running quickly; his thought processes were on high alert as he and Carl sat at the rough table. There were other tables in better condition, but all were taken with diners. The food was delicious, much like that he'd had in the many Asian countries. But he recalled with a desire almost akin to heartsickness the scrumptious foods served up from Mistress Abigail's kitchens. "Carl, do you ever hanker for heartier foods? This China food is very good, but somehow I think a bit of beef or mutton might be better preferred by the laborers. What say you?"

Shoveling a hefty forkful of the fish and rice into his mouth, Carl nodded, and finally had chewed enough to speak, "That'd be a good idea, Trenton. But where'd you find your cooks? Where'd you get your beef and mutton? In situations like where we are at present, I doubt you're gonna find anyone that will offer to let go 'the pan of gold' for the frying pan."

"You're probably right in that, but it's something to think about. And speaking of thinking... I really need your trustworthy help in a tremendous need I've encountered."

"Sounds intriguing, Trenton. I'm all ears, as the saying goes."

"Been doing a little panning myself when Sewatee and I find ourselves at the stream on my property. As you know, we get our water and we fish there. A few weeks back we both saw a few specks of the metal caught in some stone crevices. We began to pick them up, and ever since we just bring the pans along to sift through the sands while we're down there. I have accumulated a good bit of the stuff but don't know which 'blowers' are the most trustworthy. I'd hate to lose because of some dishonest person, and I know there are plenty of them around these parts. Do you have any faith in anyone? Someone you'd recommend?"

Sitting quietly, Carl gazed into Ryan's face. "Yes, friend, I myself have a small stake which is tended to by a family that I installed there. My scales are balanced. I trust only myself to weigh the metal. I give the family fifty percent of their haul. It's a paying enterprise for both of us."

"Where do you hold your wealth?"

"It's kept by a Mister Brannan in his bank down in San Francisco. Seems to be about the only place one can feel secure to amass one's gleanings. Also, I have my personal agent, a lawyer by the name of Simon Dickens. Once the value of the metal is reached, Mister Dickens, with two body guards, arrives to convey my gold, and that which belongs to my claim partner to San Francisco."

"Aren't you in fear the group may be set upon by robbers as they head back?"

"No," smiled Carl. "When you meet these three men, no one would ever suspect what they do for a living. I'm anxious for you to meet them, Trenton."

"I, as well, am anxious to make their acquaintance. And, Carl, I am truly honored that you'd trust me with this vital and critical information concerning your endeavors. Need I assure you that your confidence in me is completely secure? I feel as though I can easily confide in your integrity. Thank you."

"As soon as we finish up here, we'll head back to the office and I'll disclose all the particulars for you to make a decision as to whether or not you want to be counted in on my little endeavor. There are so few, Trenton, that can trusted. But having watched and dealt with you over the past months, and being what I consider a most honorable and decent man, my head and my heart assure me that you are indeed one of those rare men. May we both enrich our purses as well as our friendship." Carl extended his hand and as Ryan took it, placing his left hand over the clasp, Carl did the same thing.

• • •

A few weeks later, Ryan made the return journey from his cave home down to confer with Carl. This trip was planned because Attorney Simon Dickens, along with Frederick and Williams, were scheduled to be there. Upon arriving at Carl's office that morning, Ryan was surprised to enter and find three bedraggled pan-handlers seated with Carl. Wondering exactly who they were, and if he needed to hold off on bringing out the package of gold nuggets held beneath his buckskin shirt, Carl quickly stood, as did the three men. "Welcome, Trenton. Come, meet my agent, Lawyer Simon Dickens, and his sidekicks, John Frederick and Chester Williams."

Reaching forth with a handshake for each of the men, he said, "Pleased to meet you, gentlemen. I count it my great pleasure to meet you. My name is Ryan Alexander Trenton. You may call me Trenton. Most folks do."

"Ryan Alexander Trenton! So! I finally get to know your full name," said Carl.

"R. A. T. Being as how my initials say 'Rat,' I'd be just as pleased if you'd care to call me that. I was given that moniker by a most beloved woman back in London when I was just a tyke."

The men shook hands all around and finally Carl moved all the chairs together into a small circle in front of his large table. "Now that we're all on friendly terms, I believe Trenton has some questions and concerns to pose to us. Is that correct?"

Ryan nodded, and drew in a quick breath to try to gather his thoughts before exposing his open soul to these veritable strangers. He'd made up his mind that he had to trust someone, and that someone was Carl Landry. If this was a mistake he'd live to regret, then so be it. He had gotten to the place where the gold was doing nothing but giving him sleepless nights. Time had arrived when he must act if ever he was to realize his dreams. "Gentlemen. The cave where I make my home with eight souls from the Miwok tribe holds three large veins of gold. I've been systematically removing it little by little. I lied to Carl, here..." quickly acknowledging his friend, "telling him I'd been panning the stream below my property." Looking at Carl, he said, "I apologize friend, but I lied for fear you could not be trusted with the truth of the size of the lode."

Glancing at the countenances of the four men, and noting the utter surprise evidenced, he went on. "I need to set up an account whereby I may fulfill my long-range plans. You see, I have hopes of either buying or building a hotel here in Coloma, and getting my Miwok family to run it for me. Change has irrevocably arrived and this family—what's left of their tribe—is totally dependent upon me for their safety. I need to educate them in the ways of their new environment. I do not plan to remain in the mountain cave forever. And I want to bring the Miwoks out with me." Ryan slid back into his chair. It wasn't until that moment that he realized he'd been pressed forward in the chair toward his audience.

Silence. Finally, Carl spoke. "Boy, you certainly know how to play the part you chose. You had me completely fooled. I figured you to be someone completely given to the Indian way of existence. Trapping, hunting, living totally off the land. I would never have thought you had a grain of desire to become civilized. As if living in Coloma could be considered civilized!" The men all laughed at that bit of sage consideration. "Seeing as how you have become so adept at portraying the mountain man, Trenton, I now have a suspicion that your life has been even more colorful than what I can imagine."

"I don't know about colorful, but it's been interesting. I was born in London and taken aboard an American merchant ship. That's how I came to California."

"So you were a sailor, Trenton! How long were you at sea?" asked Simon.

"I was aboard the *Narcissus* under Captain Confidence Witherspoon for nigh on eleven years. I'd attained the rank of first mate before we came to San Francisco. But I need to assure you that I am now very content to be landlocked. Even though I continue to desire to move on to experience other places. I guess one could consider me to be an adventurer of sorts." His companions nodded in silent understanding.

"So now I figure I'm ready to advance the plans I have for my life. That is, as soon as we can begin to determine the value of the gold I have with me and of that yet to be realized from the cave."

Rising, Carl strode to the back of his office and brought forth a large balance as well as a box containing assorted weights. Taking a handkerchief from his pocket, he wiped the pans as well as the weights and centered the balance on his desk top.

RAT

Ryan opened his buckskin jacket and reached inside the heavy shirt to withdraw a long, narrow leather pouch. He laid it carefully on the table next to the scale. All three men leaned forward to stare wide-eyed at the size of the pouch. Carl immediately figured it weighed at least two pounds. Pulling over a good-sized sheet of paper, he held the bag over the paper and carefully untied the end. Reaching inside he began to draw out chunks of gold the size of peas. Scooping up a few he placed them onto one side of the balance. As the weight dropped down little by little, Carl placed one of the weights onto the other plate. In order to balance the trays, he had to add two more weights. Finally he removed a few nuggets until the pointer was centered. Thus far Trenton saw there was ten ounces. It was removed onto a tightly woven square of fabric. Dipping the pen into the ink well, Frederick wrote the amount of "10 oz." into a small book.

Carl continued to weigh the nuggets until all that was remaining inside the pouch was mostly dust. This last was shaken out onto the paper and weighed thusly with the total addition in the book. This present amount of gold totaled out at 29 ounces. The book was slid over to Ryan where he checked it over and in agreement signed the top and bottom of the page where nothing could be added or taken away. The full amount of gold was 39 ounces.

"Our men will leave before dawn and we can expect to hear from Mr. Brannan within one week as to the value of your new account. Every time you come down from your mountain, you can bring any gold you want weighed and I can hold it securely here in my safe until my men return for the next trip. Is this agreeable to you, Trenton?"

Ryan stood and held out his hand. "Yes, indeed. You have certainly taken a heavy burden from my shoulders. I feel like I'm going to be successful in going forward with the plans for myself and my family. I bid you gentlemen good night. I'm heading over to the hotel for a good night's sleep. I want to get out early tomorrow, and I pray you men," he glanced at the three travelers, "have a safe and uneventful journey back to San Francisco."

69

"Oh, they'll be staying at the stable for a little rest and then will start out well before dawn."

Chapter IX

C arl looked up as Ryan stood and shook off as much of the wetness as possible before entering the office. He stood and went to greet his friend. The men shook hands. "You're back sooner than I expected, Trenton. But I'm happy to see you. Does your presence today mean you've brought a new supply of your diggings for weighing?"

"Yes, and I also wanted to see if you've had news from your agent Dickens. It's been long enough surely. Nearly three weeks since our initial contract for their services. Heard anything?"

"I'm very sorry to say that I have not! I've begun to think something dire has occurred since I sent them off from here with the gold. In fact, just this morning I've contracted with two new men from the Investigative Agency of Pinkerton to see if they can ascertain exactly what has transpired with our couriers. Presently they are taking breakfast at the hotel and ought to be back within the hour."

"It isn't that I don't trust you or the Pinkerton folks, but since the fate of my family is in jeopardy, would it greatly upset you if I did some investigating on my own?"

"Why, absolutely not! Do whatever you feel you can accomplish concerning this matter! I applaud your decision, Trenton."

Ryan reached into his shirt just above his belt and withdrew the long, narrow pouch. Handing it to Carl, he said, "Keep this in your safe for me. I don't want something to happen to it while I'm travelling. Don't want to hold myself under control. Time is flying… I must do the same."

Reaching to shake Carl's hand, Ryan turned back toward the door. "I'll return quickly. I'm going back to the mountain to fetch Sewatee. We will need to glean as much information from you as you may or may not realize you possess. We will want to know everything you can recall of your conversations with Dickens and his sidekicks. Hopefully, that will provide us with enough fodder to track the interfering culprits. See you very soon."

Leaving Carl's office, Ryan split the air between two men headed toward the door he'd just vacated. He left off any attempt at civility and picked up speed.

•   •   •

Late the following evening, Carl glanced up from the dinner he'd had delivered to his office by the Chinese cook from the Hotel Coloma. With fork halfway to his gaping mouth, he jumped with fear as two unidentifiable men quickly made their way toward him.

"Hold still, Carl! It's me and Sewatee!"

"Oh my God, Trenton! I did not know who in the world was out to get me! Thank God it's you." Carl continued, "Here, back here into the back room." He motioned to the door. "Go on back, and wait until I lock up and douse the lights."

Ryan and Sewatee entered the dark room and stood until they heard Carl enter and close the door. "Hold on while I light the lantern." Fumbling around in the inky blackness of the room, the only sounds that could be heard were the heavy breathing of three nervous men. At last Carl got the lantern up and flaring and placed it on a hook suspended from a ceiling beam. "Sit." Taking a deep breath, Carl continued. "Trenton, introduce your father to me, please."

"Yes. This man holds the name of Sewatee, and is the patriarch of the family. He speaks and understands English so everything that is said between us is common knowledge to us three."

Carl reached to shake hands with Sewatee, but the old man sat silently. Sitting back down, Carl began relating everything he knew concerning the travels of his agent and two body guards. For over an hour the three men sat in a question and answer exchange. Only Sewatee never spoke. Finally, Ryan asked, "The Pinkerton men, when did they leave Coloma heading to San Francisco? Do you know anything about the tracking procedures they may use?"

"They left last night in the pouring rain. I begged them to wait, but they would not. I don't see how in the world anyone could hope to find a needle in a wet haystack." Carl smiled at his poor humor. Sewatee and Ryan did not.

Standing, Ryan reached to clasp the hand of his nervous friend and said, "Rest tonight, Carl, and pray for the safety of the Pinkerton agents as well as for Sewatee and me. We'll be on our way without any delay."

"Are you on horseback?"

"On foot."

Chapter X

L aying side by side in the deep woods, watching the encampment near the bank on the American River, Sewatee and Ryan breathed shallowly. Tempering their bodies to shut down and literally disappear. They had lain thus since just after the midnight hour. Four men lay near the bank snoring deeply all the while. Their horses had been led off hours ago; the little mule loaded with their earthly goods had been tied down near the river where she could drink her fill and munch the fresh grass; out of sight, out of mind. Ryan suspected she was packed with whatever gold they had stolen. Probably much more than his and Carl's alone.

One of the men raised up and coughed. Rising, he staggered off to the edge of the clearing to relieve himself. Sewatee gagged him and dragged his struggling body off into the darkness. Within a few minutes, another man rolled over, sat up, and said, "Wake up, you fools! Time's a wastin'. We need to git outa here before them men rise up outa th' clay an come after us!" He laughed and coughed a wet, rattling sound. As he stood and turned, Ryan laid his cocked pistol into the man's open mouth. "Don't make a sound, friend... Step this way." Ryan backed him out of the packed grass into the dark, where Sewatee took over. Ryan could hear only gruntings and thumpings behind him. Going back toward the other two snoring men, Ryan leaned over and, with his firearm laid into the ear of the third smelly man, he cocked the gun. The man's eyes flew open and Ryan said, "Make one sound and you're dead. Understand?"

He nodded as Ryan had him rise. Shoving him off toward where Sewatee was waiting, the man soon was grabbed and constrained. Returning to the last of the sleeping men, Ryan kicked him in the side and grabbed him as he scrambled upright. "Wha? What's goin' on here?"

"You'll know soon enough." With the cocked pistol held to his scruffy head, Ryan walked him into the woods where his companions were gagged and tied securely to trees. In the early morning darkness, it was still difficult for the men to glean what had happened to them. Soon the light of the sunrise would provide them with all the answers they'd want.

Sewatee prepared a meal for himself and Ryan, and as they sat and ate, the sun made itself known, even into the deep woods. No sound came from the men tethered to the trees. Each man had been situated at a tree where he could not view his companions, and thus fought little against his bonds. Not being able to speak, let alone swallow, with throats stuffed full of vile leather wads, each man sucked breaths of air through their flared nostrils, while wondering exactly what had occurred.

"What do you propose to do, Ryan?" Sewatee asked.

"Thought I'd question each one separately as to what happened to the Pinkerton agents. I fear they killed and buried them somewhere. I'll just have to see about that. If that's the case, and we've found our gold on the donkey, we may just leave them where we have them at the present time. You will remain here to see they are not disturbed, while I go on to San Francisco with the gold. I just hope the weights and names of the owners of that cache are in each bag. We'll soon find out. Eat up and let's get to it."

As Ryan had hoped, the bags of gold were undisturbed and held his name, that of Carl, and of the family who shared in his stake, as well as the weights in each bag. There was literally a lifetime fortune carried on the back of the little donkey. Ryan released the small animal and hefted the gold into a blanket roll which he had Sewatee tie across his shoulders. "It ought not take me over three days to make the round trip down to

San Francisco. Two days there, and one day to return. It will be easier to trace my way back with a much lighter load than I have going. You can expect me back anytime within the week."

"What comfort do I give to our friends?" Sewatee indicated the four prisoners with a smiling nod.

"Why, nothing. Give them no aid whatsoever. If they soil themselves, so be it. Just situate yourself upwind! It won't kill them to suffer a little. They will be more ready to answer my queries when I return. We must find out what transpired with the Pinkerton men." Ryan reached to grasp Sewatee's shoulders, and then touched his hand to Sewatee's heart and then to his own. He turned and left.

• • •

Sewatee moved the horses and led them to the river where the donkey was tethered. He tied them there so they too could tear loose the green tufts of sweet grasses and drink their fill of water. Returning to the stamped-down circle of the camp site, Sewatee set about sweeping away all remnants of the men's presence. He relocated himself into the crotch of a large leafed oak tree uphill from where the campsite had been. From his vantage point he could see the contented animals as well as the discontented prisoners. Neither men nor animals were aware of where he was comfortably ensconced.

The daylight hours passed quickly for Sewatee as he dozed on and off. Taking no time to eat nor relieve himself, he simply enjoyed this respite from civilization, listening to the sounds of nearby birds and passing wildlife. None of which were interested in the men nor livestock tethered nearby. As night came on, he sighed and nodded securely into a restful sleep.

Waking at the slight sound of a nicker by one of the horses, Sewatee could see by the moonlight that there appeared to be a puma sniffing toward the place where the animals were held. As yet the cat had not reached the point where it could view the tethered creatures. Sewatee dropped silently to the soft earth and, with knife in hand, approached the cat with equal stealth. The yellow eyes turned slowly toward the strange animal headed toward it. With cunning, the cat tried intimidation with a slow snarl.

Sewatee opened his throat and let out a scream to raise the hair on the neck of the puma, as well as fill the prisoners with awesome fear! Without further ado, the puma turned tail and ran off quickly down the riverside toward parts unknown. Sobbing through their slobber, the four men trembled in imagined horror of what they knew was their fate at the fangs of some banshee. Sewatee grinned as he silently strode by them back to the big oak. They never knew he was there.

•   •   •

Walking into the now-nonexistent camp site, Ryan saw the four pitiful souls whimpering at the base of the trees. Before he could turn, Sewatee was beside him. "Here, Ryan, eat. You are back sooner than even I expected. What did you do? All the business taken care of?"

Sitting down on a fallen log, Ryan ate ravenously while relating the news to his father. "Yes, I set up the account for us as well as turned over the other gold to a Mister Brannan. He owns the bank there. He recognized the other depositors and applied the value to each one. I have the receipts here." He patted his shirt. "I'll give them to Carl when we get back to Coloma." Looking around, he spied the desperate men. Still tied in place but much the worse for wear. They stunk to high heaven, and Ryan had never seen more miserable humans in his life.

"As soon as I finish, I'll get right to finding out what, if anything, they did to those Pinkerton men. Mr. Brannan confirmed that none of the five ever arrived there, so they were waylaid between Coloma and there. Come, let us find out."

Ryan stooped in front of the man nearest to where he had eaten his breakfast. "I'm going to ask you some very simple questions. You will answer them. All. You will not be allowed freedom until I'm satisfied that you have given me the truth. Do you understand?"

The man nodded as deeply as possible, then held still. Sewatee removed the sopping leather wad from the man's mouth. Ryan laid a finger against his own lips and said, "Make no sound until I request your cooperation. Now, give the names of your companions in crime. Speak."

"The oldest is my brother, Herbert. Herbert Whittle. The other two are my cousins. My mama's sister's boys. They's Ralph and his brother Peter Millwood."

Nodding, Ryan smiled. "And now for your name…"

"It's Foster Whittle. Whatcha gonna do—"

Ryan motioned for Sewatee to cram the leather back into his mouth. "I told you to not speak unless I asked you directly. What I'm about to do will depend on what I find out from your kin, tied to yonder trees."

Between Ryan and Sewatee, through none too gentle prodding, they uncovered the full truth of what the men had done. They had religiously dogged the agents from Coloma for two days before they finally took action and robbed them. The men had been tied and taken to the Millwood house situated on the American River not five miles from where the thieves were now being held. It was there that the three men were murdered and buried on the property next to the house. The two Pinkerton men had been noisily making their way toward where the fresh graves were when they were set upon and murdered by the four thieves. They were buried in the clay bank, downstream from where the Millwoods panned for gold.

Ryan and Sewatee left the four men tied to the trees where they'd spent the last several days. As they mounted their horses, leading two and the little donkey, Ryan lifted his hat in farewell toward the four hapless prisoners. Leaving them there to die was more than what they deserved. Maybe the hungry puma would return to feed, or it was just possible that some family member from upriver might stumble upon them before they finally did perish. It was better odds than they'd given the five men they'd murdered.

•   •   •

Arriving back in Coloma, Ryan loaded Sewatee with fresh supplies to take on ahead to their mountain home. Ryan then made his way to Carl's office. Noting the door was firmly locked, he hoped he might find him ensconced at a table in the hotel. It was, after all, near dinner time. He strode over, entered the lobby, and glanced into the dining room. Gladly, he spied Carl at a heavily-laden table, sitting with another man, one Ryan did not know. Without hesitation, Ryan approached the pair and spoke. "Carl, as you can see, I've returned. May I join you?"

Swinging his hand magnanimously toward a vacant chair, Carl replied, "Paul, let me introduce you to my good friend, Mr. Trenton. Trenton, this is Paul Robertson. New in town and desiring to open his law offices here. I'm yet to talk him into sharing my office space. I've more than enough room and it would surely be right handy to have a legal mind close by."

Paul rose slightly, leaned across the table, and met Ryan's grip. The men were not bashful in their piercing gaze into the eyes of the other. Ryan often measured a man by his eye contact. He quickly came to the conclusion that Paul was a trustworthy and straightforward kind of man. Desiring to know more, Ryan asked, "Do you have family here with you?"

"Why, no sir, I do not. My wife, Shirley is back East and will join me as soon as I've settled and prepared a place worthy of her. So far, the area hereabouts leaves much to be desired for my decision to bring her and our new son out here. She is safe with her parents in Boston."

"Wonderful. I do hope the plans I have for Coloma may soon make it possible for you—not just you—but many responsible citizens to settle here." Then turning to Carl, he said, "I have news, Carl. Good and bad. As soon as you're ready we must get back to your office."

"I'm anxious to know your news, Trenton. May our new friend Paul be privy to our meeting? I believe he may just be able to guide our endeavors with more ease than we've had in past... But, here now. Do you want a meal before we go?"

"No. Sewatee and I ate not long before we got back. He's gone back up to the mountain with new supplies for the family."

"You'll have to bring Paul up to date on your holdings and your family. Come, gentlemen. Let us pay our tab and get out of here."

•   •   •

The telling of it all elicited a myriad of expressions from the faces of both Carl and Paul. "Well, at least now we know what became of our friends. We'll have Paul write up reports to be sent to the agencies involved. With that sad news it places quite a damper upon my elation about the recovery of all the stolen gold. The family who trusts me to get their gold to the bank will be very relieved to now know of its safety. Thank you for bringing the deposit slips back. I just dread passing along the news of five murdered men. You're sure the culprits are receiving their just reward for such doings?"

"I think you have no need of worry concerning them. They were already half gone by the time Sewatee and I left them. They'd been without food or water for nearly a week, and by now have either become several meals for the puma or the blowflies. But for your peace of mind, I will check on them the next time I head to San Francisco with our gold. Until you can contract with a new agent for the trip, I'll be more than happy to make the trips for you."

"Say, Trenton, that's a great idea. Since you'll be taking it, there won't be any reason for you to pay for its transfer." He grinned toward Paul.

•   •   •

Every few weeks, Ryan made the trip to San Francisco on foot. Deciding he'd rather walk the trip than take a horse, he could keep completely out of sight, travelling through the woods, alternating his path each time. The initial trip took him by the place where the four thieves-murderers were tied. All were dead. Something had halfheartedly eaten at one of them, then apparently found it less than palatable and left. The condors and flies were having themselves a veritable concert while gnawing away at the rotting flesh. Ryan was glad to be away from the terrible sight. Even though the men had given no mercy to those whom they'd murdered, it was still a sorry end to God's created beings. On subsequent trips Ryan never went by there again.

• • •

Carl had, at last, contracted with two new men to courier the gold from Coloma. He'd queried them extensively, together and separately, to glean some assurance as to their honesty. One, Jeffry Hallback, recently arrived with his young family, and the other Arthur Albertson, a photographer from New York. Arthur agreed to the job simply because he needed the money and the trips would give him ample opportunity to photograph this new country. Both the men, as well as Carl, knew this arrangement would be short-lived, but it would have to do until better replacements could be found. So few able-bodied men were available. Everyone was still panning for the golden goddess, dreaming of riches beyond all good sense.

• • •

One afternoon, after a particularly boring meal, Ryan and Carl found themselves seated on a low bench in front of the hotel, soaking in the warmth of the sun and drowsing in contentment. However, Ryan's thought processes were raging within his mind. *I think I've found my place in life now. My destiny is fulfilled!* "Carl!"

Jumping, somewhat, Carl asked, "What?"

"I'm going to offer for this hotel. I heard Millburn talking when we were eating that he wanted to set up in San Francisco. Don't know if he has any idea of selling out or if he just wants to put someone in charge here. Whatcha think?"

"How would I know, Trenton? All you gotta do is go in and ask him. And by the way, where'd this hare-brained idea come from anyways?"

"Well, you know I've planned for a while now to come live in Coloma and bring my family with me. If I get the hotel, I can fix it up like I'd like to see a good hotel done, and get Wauna and the girls cooking and cleaning. Until I can find someone trustworthy to run the mine, I'd leave Sewatee and the boys up there."

"Trenton, go on in and find Millburn. In fact, I'll come with you. Okay?"

"Sure, you can steer me right if I begin to head off on some rabbit trail!" He laughed.

•   •   •

Paul Robertson drew up the papers and Ryan Alexander Trenton found himself the new owner of a two story ramshackle building.

Ryan set to work immediately hiring carpenters to work on his new hotel. He sent into all the surrounding areas for men to come work. He made each one sign a contract that stipulated that if anyone left without reason, all work done up to that point would be considered a gift to him. Ryan soon had several good men that could follow his design directions, and within a few weeks of travel back and forth to San Francisco for supplies, Ryan was delighted to witness a real honey of a hotel taking shape.

A nicely boarded walkway was installed, which sported two benches, one on either side of the glass topped doors. Inside, it featured a decent lobby on one side with stairs leading up to the second floor rooms, and on the left side of the double-door entrance he located the long bar on the far side of the dining room. Kitchens, laundry, and bath houses were situated in the rear across a boarded alleyway. Beyond that were large pens holding the animals for slaughter. Ryan wanted real beef and mutton and pork to offer his dining patrons. He hired a family of Chinese to do the hotel laundry and take care of the bath houses. Two families of Mormons took over the slaughtering and meat storage. The houses for these workers were between where they worked and the fine little stream running beyond down into a cool wooded area.

Another group of settlers were living in temporary houses of tin and canvas until better could be produced. They supplemented their living by selling fresh grown produce to the kitchen master, Dalton Hobbs.

Ryan was now ready to make what he hoped would be his final trip up to the cave. He arrived late one evening to find his family all asleep. At his unexpected entrance, he felt a whale of a whip across the back of his legs, easily knocking him to the ground with a loud *whoomph*! Within seconds, and in the inky blackness, Sewatee had him blindfolded and trussed. Ryan lay unmoving while he waited for a lantern to be lit. "Oh, Ryan, it's you! Here," said Pakuma, "Let me untie you. Why you come so late, and not for a long time? You did not know we set traps for such as you coming in the night."

"I'm sorry, Pakuma. It appears I've been with the white man too long and have forgotten my good sense."

"Welcome home, my son," said Sewatee. "Sit here and have some good stew. You losing some of yourself from being so long with the whites."

"I guess you're right. I've been doing a lot since we last were together. That's what I've come now to speak with you all about."

"Tell us what you want of us, son, and we shall comply. You have been our chief for many moons and have taken care of your family... more than even some of our own people would have done. Let us hear now what you have on your heart."

Without too much diversion, Ryan explained that he desired for Wauna, Pakuma, and the girls—Huata, Sanuye, and Kamata—to come live in the building in Coloma to care for it and the people who would be coming to stay and take meals there. It would be easy work; there would be no need for much foraging for foods as most would be handy. He continued and explained that Sewatee and the boys—Oya and Tukuli—

would continue to keep the cave and mine going until Ryan could either bring them down to live and work in Coloma, or else stay there along with another family yet to be found.

There was a very long silence before Sewatee finally spoke. "What you desire is not a happy thing, but it is a necessary thing. Especially for the women. They must someday accept the upheaval that has taken over this world in which we live, and the time has come when they must alter their living to merge into this new life. They will prepare to return to Coloma with you when you are ready. Oya and Tukuli will remain here with me until we decide what we must do. Now, get your rest. I have several packets of gold for you to take back tomorrow."

"Thank you, father. I shall unpack the supplies I brought then, too."

•   •   •

Sitting in the sunshine outside his office, Carl watched as Ryan walked into Coloma with a pack mule carrying an Indian woman and a young girl, his horse loaded with two more girls, and one beautiful girl walking beside him. *Guess Trenton went to get his family after all.*

"I'll be over to see you as soon as I get my family settled in. On second thought, Carl, how about you come over for supper in about an hour or so? We can talk over steaks," called Ryan.

"That's a promise! See you in a while." Carl rose and went into his musty office to finish some work he'd been putting off.

Chapter XI

S till on the lookout for just the right man to work his claim, Ryan
stayed vigilant. To his way of thinking, the man must be needy
enough to want to work and honest enough to be trusted. What with the
constant influx of immigrants to the gold fields, Ryan was hoping to
fulfill his desire with just the right person. He'd know him when he saw
him.

A few days later found Ryan stepping out through the heavy double
doors and pausing in the late afternoon sunlight to let his eyes adjust. A
large bustling arose from the east end of the street as another wagon
creaked, clanged, and lumbered into the settlement of Coloma. The
wagon team was being handled by a small sandy-haired boy. A hollow-
eyed woman was sitting behind him holding a bundle to her chest. Ryan
could see a raft of faces peering out from behind the two on the forward
seat. A ragged man was trudging alongside a starving cow and two mules.
The only creatures of this ensemble that looked none the worse for wear
were a couple of goats, a billy and a nanny.

Ryan watched, now intensely interested. Their plight brought to his
memory his own near starvation and poverty. He stepped off the boards
and extended his hand to the man. He was greeted with a snag-toothed

smile, that looked for the world like the mug of a snarling dog. "My name's Ryan Trenton, sir. Welcome to Coloma," Ryan said.

Taking the proffered hand in a weak grasp, the traveler replied, "Thanks, Mister Trenton. Frank Martin here," then sweeping his arm expansively, "and this is my family, home, and stock."

"Again, welcome, sir."

"You can call me Frank."

"Yes, sir, Frank. Once you're settled in a bit, I'd count it my pleasure to treat you and your missus and chaps to you first meal in my hotel."

"Great fires o' hell, Mister Trenton…"

"You can call me Ryan."

"Okay, Ryan! Whatcha wanna do that for? We don't take to charity! We take care of our own by ourselves!"

Ryan realized this was a very prideful, but very needy, gentleman he was dealing with. *Better be humble and gentle here.* "No, sir, Frank. Not charity at all. I've been here long enough to know that sometimes everyone could use some friendship. All I'm offering is my friendship and the desire to aid you in whichever way you might want. That's all. Really."

"Umm, in that case, I suppose the family could use a rest somewhat before we have to locate a place to bed down for the night."

"The livery is right behind that shop up at the end of the street, yonder," said Ryan with a forward nod of his head. "Then there's Mrs. Quincy's boarding house over this way." He gestured back toward the far edge of the town.

"Oh, we won't be a needin' any of that. We're self-contained… got it all right here." Frank patted the ragged canvas of his bedraggled wagon.

Ryan could hear the whimpering of children from inside the wagon and noticed the dead silence of the bundle in Mrs. Martin's arms. His gut wrenched to witness the staunch pride of this man before him. Ryan knew he had to proceed carefully with the plans he had in mind. He didn't want to lose this opportunity. "Yes sir, I know, I know. And a fine rig you do have. Bless God, this has served you and your family well along your travels. You're a lucky man to get here with all your family intact."

Frank dropped his head. "Would that we had, Mr. Ryan."

Ryan noticed the "mister" tacked onto his name and hoped that meant that Frank was giving him enough respect as to begin to heed his upcoming offers.

Frank continued, "No, we buried two of our'n coming on, and Callie birthed another. We had six head, lost two, gained one, so we now have five looking to me for life. Me and Callie gonna do good by our chaps, too. But we're hoping to put the two older children out to work... That's Millicent and Johnny. The two younger ones, that's Patricia and Monroe. They'll be staying with us. We gotta get busy finding a stake to make our fortune. After all, that's the real reason we come out here."

Ryan countered with, "Mr. Frank, let me get you started with one night in my hotel. That'll at least give you all one night of rest. Y'all can get baths and sleep in real beds for a change... and then we can have a chance to talk some." Hesitating, then continuing, "If you have to pull out'a town to set up camp, it'll be more difficult for us to talk. How about it?"

Frank didn't have to even look up; he could feel the silent pleas of his children permeating his skin, and he knew Callie needed some attention with the new babe. With a quick nod, he said, "You'll be paid back twict over, Ryan." And he extended his hand.

Leading the way, Ryan helped get the children herded toward the door while Frank lifted his wife and newborn down to the boardwalk. "The wife, she's not doing so well. The babe been born two days back and she ain't let go of it since then. The little thing ain't cried hardly at all. Least ways not though this whole day it ain't."

"Frank, may I see to stabling your horses and cattle in the livery? They'll be tended to and fed. Sonny here can take the wagon down to the end of the street for safekeeping. His pa runs the livery. The tabs on me. You're my guest."

"Now, I don't mean to get all suspicious on you or nothin', but why'd you want to do all this for a bunch of strangers?"

"I can see right off that you're a man that uses his head. That alone makes me admire your leadership. Why, you've accomplished so much in just getting your family out to Coloma. You deserve some recognition for your efforts. And I can use such a one as yourself ... But we'll speak of that over dinner. What do you say we get your family into their rooms. Get yourselves cleaned up a bit... Wipe some of that trail dust away and get comfortable."

Entering Hotel Coloma, the incongruous group elicited few notices. The little town burgeoned with all sorts. None attracted much attention.

Attorney Paul Robertson was coming out of the lobby as Ryan and Frank entered through the wide double doors. Ryan stopped Paul with a touch to his arm. "Can I talk with you soon? You gonna stay here in town for the next few days?"

"Sure. Whatcha need?"

"Your advice and expertise. I'll come by your room or else I'll send word when I'm free. When we do get together, I'll know by then more what I'm wanting to do."

"Okay, I'll be in town at least two and probably three more weeks before I head out again."

"Great, that'll give me plenty of time to firm up the plans."

The men parted with a handshake, and Ryan turned to Sonny, who was seated on the boards. He flipped him a small coin that glinted brightly as it arced in the air and hit the waiting palm. "Stay right there until I get back. I've got a job for you."

"Sure, Mister T."

•   •   •

Frank was leaning heavily against the lobby desk, looking as though he was ready to collapse at any second. Ryan hurried to his side and quickly slid his hand across the polished wooden counter top toward the nattily dressed and barbered man behind it. "You'll have two rooms and baths for Ryan Trenton!"

The man, recently hired for this position of desk clerk, and soon to be fired if he didn't do better than this, jumped as if he'd been slapped. "Yes sir! Mr. Trenton! I just didn't recognize you, sir. I was day dreaming I guess. I'm sorry, sir…"

"Everyone is allowed one mistake when new on the job. Don't let this kind of inattention ever happen again, Gilbert." Continuing, Ryan said, "Get the keys to rooms four and five, and have two baths brought up to the rooms. "

"Right away, sir."

Frank looked at Ryan with new interest. Who was this young man, anyway, and what in blazes did he have to do with himself?

"Go on up, Frank. I'll get the missus and your flock and have whatever the wife says you'll need sent right up."

With a ragged gasp, Frank let go of the tight strings that had held him together across that endless trek, and as he turned and trudged up the stairs following Thomas, his eyes dropped great silent tears of relief.

The eldest child, Millicent, touched Ryan's arm as they passed, and she said, "I'll go with you and tell you where everything is that's to be brought up to our rooms. Mama isn't able right now."

Ryan and the girl returned to the front of the hotel where young Sonny was flipping the gold coin high into the air to watch as it sparkled brightly before dropping quickly back into his dirty hand.

"Come."

Together the three dug through and removed the trunks and baskets containing the needed belongings. Once the necessary baggage was offloaded, Ryan sent Sonny off with the remainder of the scant possessions still in the odorous wagon, followed closely by the livestock, to the livery stable.

Enlisting the help of a pair of passersby to quickly carry the creaking trunks up the stairs, Ryan led, with his right hand in the small of Mrs. Martin's back for support, up to room four. "Ma'am, you and your children will be alright. I'm sending for our town's doctor to come by real soon to help you and the babe."

Callie made no sound or acknowledgement of what was said. She was on her last vestige of strength as she silently climbed the stairs. Four equally silent children were close behind them. Frank was standing at the open door of a room on the left of the wide hallway. He came to lead his wife, still clutching the silent bundle tightly to her bosom, into the room.

Ryan sent the boys into their parent's room which contained two large beds. They watched as a large copper tub was being filled by the kitchen help. Millicent and Patricia were shown into a smaller room across the hall where another tub was waiting. Ryan told them, as he closed the door, "I'll send for you in about an hour. Meantime, gather all the clothes to be laundered and set them at the top of the stairs. Then get bathed and be ready to come downstairs for supper."

Ryan woke the napping Chaing and his crew to set the water to boiling for the laundry he'd be sending out in just a little while.

·   ·   ·

"Seen doc lately?" asked Ryan.

"Yes sir. Doctor Jonas, he left about an hour ago headed to the mortician's house," said Sonny, pointing in the direction, as if Ryan didn't know where it was.

"How about you fetch Whistler for me, Sonny."

"Sure thing. Be back in a jiffy." As Sonny ran off toward the livery stable, Ryan went back inside to alert his crew to prepare a generous meal for the family ensconced upstairs. He also told them he was going to fetch Doctor Jonas to see about the lady. "You take care of everything, Wauna. I'll be back soon."

Clive was the same age as Ryan and had come into the area at about the same time. Clive had actually never intended to search for gold, but being the business-minded man that he was, he set about immediately to getting a wood shop built for the large box of tools he'd brought. As the shop building was completed, he began his chosen trade—that of casket maker and mortician.

As he earned the money, he built his home. And a fine one it proved to be. Clive had soon found a wife in one of the young women of a group of camp followers. Gertrude was ecstatic over her good fortune as the wife of a real honest-to-God professional man. And being the mistress of her own fine home at the west end of the settlement was satisfying in every way.

No one in Coloma was considered an outcast or beneath another. They were all "an assortment of vegetables in the same stew", as Reverend Cantrell always said.

Ryan reined in at the front of the house, but as he tethered Whistler, he heard voices and laughter coming from around back where the shop was located. Clive and Jonas were in a jovial conversation and, upon seeing Ryan rounding the back corner of the house, they stepped forward together to greet him. "How you doin', Ryan? What brings you here on this fine evenin'?"

Shaking hands with both men, Ryan said, "Jonas, I'd sure like you to come take a look at a lady that's in a real bad way, I think."

"Where is she?"

"At my hotel. She and her family have only just arrived and it appears to me she's not got long on this earth. The babe she birthed a couple days back is gone for sure, and I fear the lady will follow soon. But I need you to do whatever you can. She may make it with your help."

Jonas turned to bid a quick goodbye to his friend and asked that his compliments be forwarded to Missus Gertrude for the fine apple pie and coffee. He strode over and entered his buggy and pulled out of the yard, following Ryan into the fast approaching darkness.

* * *

From his vantage point in the dining room, Ryan could see Jonas descending the stairs and their eyes met. Jonas was tight-lipped and shaking his head. Ryan rose from the table and met the doctor at the base of the steps. "The baby has been dead for quite some time... I'd guess a couple days, and the lady is not likely to make it through the night. She's burning with fever. Afraid she's beyond any help I can give. I dosed her with laudanum and instructed her daughters to bathe and dress her in clean night clothes. I'll send for Clive to come for the child tonight and to get a box ready for the lady soon. If the lady doesn't rally, they can both be buried together. How about you get in touch with the reverend?"

"I'll do that now, Jonas. He ought to be here for the family." With this turn of events, Ryan felt this would secure the deal he'd had in mind for Frank and the children. But he'd wait until the proper time to speak of it.

Ultimately, Frank Martin would always feel indebted to Ryan Trenton for having been there during such times of trauma and disbelief as did, indeed, occur that fateful night. He had literally been thrown a lifeline by a perfect stranger.

By the time Clive had driven his wagon over to the hotel to fetch the babe, Doctor Jonas had pronounced Callie Martin dead. She had been dressed in a freshly-laundered gown. Wauna sat with her as her husband and children were downstairs attempting to eat. Even during times of such deep sorrow there's something comforting in sharing a meal. Quietly they consumed the foods; the only sounds were those of silverware upon china plates and the muffled sounds emanating from the kitchen at the rear of the building.

Ryan had thoughtfully seated the family facing the long bar toward the east side of the large dining room. He hoped that when the deceased ones were removed from the hotel that none of the family would be aware of the transfer of their loved ones. As it transpired, they never knew when mother and babe were taken away.

Both bodies were wrapped together in white sheets and carried down the steps and out through the big double doors and placed on a bed of straw in the rear of Clive's wagon. From there they were driven over to the little church and placed together in the pine casket set down in front of the altar until the morrow when Reverend Cantrell would see that the site out back of the church was dug and prepared to receive the box.

After Frank and the children were satiated and ready to get to bed, Ryan gathered the five close and broke the news. "I knew it, I knew it. She acted like everything was fine, but I knew it. She was too proud to let on how she was sufferin'. But she ain't sufferin' no more. Nossir, she ain't sufferin' no more." The little family wept silently and deeply. Ryan had brandy brought for Frank and a piece of fruit given to the children to keep them busy for a few more minutes.

"Tomorrow, Frank, we'll walk over to the church where Reverend Cantrell will be prepared to say a few words, or you and the children can also say anything you want. She can be buried with your little baby out back beneath the elm trees. I'll have her name carved and the dates, with whatever you want to place over where she'll rest. If that's alright."

Frank reached to grasp Ryan in a tight hug as his body shook with grief. "That'll be fine, Mr. Trenton. Just fine."

"You and the children go on upstairs now and try to rest. Mornin'll be here before we know it."

• • •

Ryan's plan of partnering was conceived to protect his already extensive fortune as well as add to it by the labors of other individuals. This would release him from the constant obligation to his holdings in Coloma and his established rights on the mountain.

By installing Frank and his boys in the mine, Sewatee, Oya, and Tukuli would be free to leave. Ryan knew that their being "tied to the cave" was not something those three were content with. They had stayed on in the cave and worked the gold only out of their love for Ryan. The gold itself meant nothing to them, except that it did allow for the security of Wauna, Pakuma, and the three younger girls in this new "white man's world", which they despised.

With his thought processes spinning rapidly, Ryan came to the conclusion that his destiny was not yet met. *I must make my way to the east of this big country. Maybe there my destiny will be fulfilled and I can build a family instead of just a fortune.* He'd been dodging the amorous advances of

Pakuma. She was a dear and beautiful young woman, but Ryan simply had no hankering to build a family here. He had a burning desire to see more of this great country. He wanted to head back east, and he hoped, with Frank's help, to be able to do just that.

•   •   •

Lawyer Paul Robertson drew up the binding contracts between Frank and Ryan, as well as the papers turning over the ownership of Hotel Coloma to Wauna and Pakuma jointly. Ryan was explaining the situation to Frank and his four children at dinner the evening before he was to lead the way up to the mine. "Frank, you and your sons will be very comfortable living there as everything is secured and well cared for. Of course Millicent and Patricia will make their way here at the hotel, working with Wauna and Pakuma to serve the guests."

"Well, Mister Ryan, I understood that you had a coupla Indians living in your cave home. What'll happen? Will we all be in there together? I don't see how that will do! I'm kinda distrustful of them people, you know?"

Nodding, Ryan said, "Yes, Frank. I understand your thoughts about this, but believe me when I tell you that Sewatee and the boys are ready to leave that place. They've been there much longer than I ever thought I could hold them. I know they're still there out of deference to me."

"Well, if you say so. I just know me and my boys'll feel much safer without them redskins in the way all the time."

Laughing, Ryan answered, "You won't need to concern yourself with that, Frank. They are very peaceful people and sweetly pliable. Why, look at how Wauna and the girls have altered their way of life here. The young ones will probably end up marrying some young miners and have a tentful of kids."

Interrupting the laughter, Millicent, Frank's oldest child, spoke up. "But, Daddy, I hate it here. I've seen how Pakuma looks at me! She does not like me at all, and I want to go back east where I can meet a husband

and raise my family there. Please, Daddy. Don't make me stay here," begged Millicent.

With Millicent being seventeen, Ryan could understand her trepidation of beginning this new, unsettled life without her mother and under the tutelage of two Indians who had become established in their own ways. "Frank, I'd be willing to see to it that Millicent gets back east. I can pay her passage as soon as the next ship sails for Boston with a shipment of gold."

Frank opened his mouth, but Millicent wailed it shut. "No! Daddy, I don't want to wait that long! Can't I just go with Mr. Trenton when he leaves?" Turning toward Ryan, she continued. "I'll not be any trouble. I can cook on the trail. I'm used to hardship. I took care of everybody coming here, especially after Mama got sick. For those last weeks I had the entire responsibility. Remember, Daddy?"

As Frank silently nodded, truly understanding his child's fearfulness at her supposed new situation, he glanced over at Ryan for some intelligent argument. But Ryan's thought processes were running every which way, seeking exit arguments. Nothing was forthcoming that would douse the fires of passion raging in Millicent's mind.

Millicent continued, "I truly will be so much help to you, Mr. Trenton. If you leave without me, pretty soon you'll be thinking to yourself: 'Now why didn't I bring Millicent with me? She sure would be a big help right about now!'"

Finally, Frank spoke up, "Child, you ain't got no idea of what you're saying! Why me and the boys will be far away, up in the hills, and you won't see us for maybe days or weeks. You gotta stay here with Patricia. She won't have anyone to be with and she sure can't go to the hills with us."

Turning to her sister, Millicent said, "You won't mind if I'm not here will you, Patty? Why you and that boy, Sonny, are already friends. I see you two all the time together. Tell Pa it'll be alright for me to go."

Imagining how great it would be without her bossy older sister, Patricia said, "Yes, Pa, let her go. I'll be fine by myself. And I really won't be by myself. I'll be working in the hotel too and running errands for everybody just like Sonny does. There'll be plenty to keep me busy, what with schooling and all."

Millicent could tell by the silence of her father that he was considering it, so she added, "If you'll just let me go, I can tell your sister and all the family all about how well you're doing here. Also it'll be better to tell them firsthand about how Ma is gone and how you and the boys are running an actual gold mine."

Ryan knew Frank was considering allowing his child to return to the family back east. But there was no way he was going to travel by wagon or coach to accommodate this young woman. His thoughts suddenly became verbalized. "Frank, I guess I'm a fool, but *if*, and I do mean *if*, I decide that Millicent should accompany me on this trip, I'd suggest we have Reverend Cantrell marry us—in name only, mind you—to alleviate any slur on Millicent's good character. As soon as we arrive wherever it is that she decides she wants to end up, we could have the arrangement annulled, and she'd be free to seek her own way. What do you say about this?"

"I'm not much of a man to want to stand in the way of my child who has been through so much already. I'll agree to it if you can get your lawyer friend to make up a little contract on top of the marriage contract sayin' that *if*, and I do mean *if*, something were to happen to my daughter—say like getting with child—that you could not put them away for any reason."

"You surprise me, Frank, but please me too! I see right off that I'm dealing with a very intelligent man, and I'd be more'n happy to oblige. In the morning I'll get Paul and Cantrell to do the honors. Would after breakfast be okay with you for the ceremony to take place?" Then to Millicent he said, "Are you agreeable to this course of action, my dear?"

Smiling broadly, she shyly nodded. "Yes sir. That'd be right nice."

• • •

That night as Ryan was alone in his room getting everything ready for the wedding tomorrow and deciding exactly what would be excess and what was absolute necessity for the trip, he felt something behind him. Turning quickly he found himself body to body with Pakuma. "What the tarnation are you doing here? What do you want?"

Without any wasted motion or moment, Pakuma reached to his manhood with both hands and simply said, "This. Ryan, give me this."

Jumping backward, he landed upon his bed and shook his head... "Are you crazy, Pakuma? I'm marrying in the morning and leaving Coloma for good. You know this is not good for either of us! I will not do this. No!" Rising from the bed, he tried to get past the insistent girl. He tried to reach the door but her hands were all over him and were busy opening his clothes. "Why in the world do you want this? You know I am leaving."

"Yes, Ryan. I know you are leaving. That is why I want this now. Please give me this part of yourself so I can hold you close in my dreams from now on. This is all that I will ever have of you."

Ryan was torn by her confession of need. He watched as tears welled up and flowed silently from her eyes. Losing all fortitude against the girl, he said, "Lock the door."

• • •

As the pocket watch resting in the hand of Reverend James Cantrell binged out ten times, the company of folks traipsed down the center aisle of the little church. Millicent was decked out in virginal white—so recently laundered and ironed by Chaing's family—and Ryan wore a severe black suit with a high-collared white shirt. The lawyer brought up the rear behind Frank, Patricia, and the boys. As the distance between them closed, James stepped forward and solemnly faced Ryan and Millicent. "Dearly beloveds, we..."

A few moments later Ryan was admonished, "You may now kiss your wife!"

While a flurry of activity assailed his ears, he quickly leaned down and placed a chaste kiss upon the upturned lips of his bride. *"HIS*

WIFE!" Lord, how in the world did this happen? And what in tarnation had happened last night? God help me.

Frank took his good time reading through the contract, and finally signing his name, he raised back up with a smile and a sigh of relief. "I know you'll take good care of her for me, won't you, *son?*"

A sudden chill rolled over Ryan as his thought processes roiled in anguish. *What have I done?*

Belying his inner turmoil, Ryan spoke. "You can count on me, Frank. I'll treat her as you would. With gentleness and honor. You can dismiss any worry about her."

Millicent Trenton held within her heart a grin too big to allow to form on her lips, which were demurely kept without emotion.

Chapter XII

Not one to let a simple wedding ceremony interfere with important plans, Ryan spoke. "Frank, anytime you and the boys are ready we can head up to the mine. Johnny and young Monroe have already packed the mule with everything, and Sonny can bring our horses whenever you say."

"Then let's us git out of these duds and into our work clothes, and send for the horses. C'mon, boys, we got daylight to burn yet!"

Everyone laughed at Frank's enthusiasm and entered the hotel as one. Millicent ran quickly up the stairs to begin her plans, with Patricia close behind. The boys headed to change clothes. They were so excited to begin the new adventure and actually dig real gold from the mine. They both expected to become wealthy and had big dreams of what they would do with their share. Ryan was castigating himself for the quandary of having to deal with the fires of desire he saw in the eyes of Millicent. He'd seen those same fires burning in Pakuma.

• • •

Luke "Wishbone" Newburn had been in Coloma only a week, spending his time propping up the bar in Sam's Saloon. "What's all the excitement about?"

"Why, the town's richest man is gittin' married this morning!"

"Zat so? Who's he hitchin' to… one of yore girls?"

"Naw. He's got a hot little filly from our latest influx of would-be gold seekers. Her ma died right when they got here and Mr. Trenton kinda took the whole family under his wing, so to speak."

"Yeah? Boy, I bet they're sure blessin' themselves to have run into such a situation. Wish I could hook up with something like that. I need a good-paying stake." He laughed. "I hope you know you just took my last dollar."

"Unh, unh. And I hope you know you had your last drink, mister! Finish up and move along. We don't need no freeloaders hanging around taking up room from the payers." Lifting the empty glass from beneath the arm of his customer, Sam wiped the bar as Luke gently staggered out through the swinging doors and onto the crowded boardwalk. Blinking in the early sunlight, he wavered slightly as he waited for his eyesight to adjust, just in time to watch the wedding party making its way toward the hotel. He headed in that direction.

Luke was bound to learn what his next course of action would be by listening to the conversations of the group just plowing through the big doors of the Hotel Coloma.

Head down, mouth shut, ears wide open. This had gotten him to where he was, and would more than likely carry his hide on into his next adventure. His emergence into the happy group was completely unnoticed. As the women stomped up the stairs, the men drew into the dining room and headed to the long bar. Luke sidled to the bar like the rest of them and waited for the heavy little glass to be slid into his waiting palm. *Nice.*

So! The greenhorns are a wantin' to head back across the vast and dangerous plains all alone. That pore fool of a man will probably be totin' plenty of gold or some sorta funds to get 'em along the way. I'll just make myself indispensable until providence gives me to go ahead to leave 'em in the dirt. Smiling, he figured 'this richest man' surely would be rich pickin's.

Luke made himself off to be an old, trusted friend of Ryan's while Ryan, Frank, and his boys were gone up into the hills. He made Millicent believe that he'd already been asked to be their guide on the upcoming trip back.

Millicent wasn't too happy about having to share her newlywed state with this utter stranger, but then she did suppose that having a seasoned guide would benefit their safety and comfort. Philosophical as she was prone to be, she totally bought into the farce set up by Luke. She must remember to thank Ryan for his forethought concerning their safety in the hiring of the man.

Chapter XIII

W ith four horses and a mule, Ryan, Millicent, and the newly-hired guide, Luke Newburn, bid the folks of Coloma farewell. "I'll keep in touch as often as I can. Paul, you and Carl hold the fort for me, and wish us Gods' speed."

•   •   •

Leading the way, Luke determined to carry the two greenhorns as far as he could to try to determine just how able-bodied they were. He wanted to test them, thereby he'd learn what it would take to get them so worn out until, when the time presented itself, he could easily take what he wanted and leave them to fend for themselves in some godforsaken area.

The little party had been out for some five hours when Ryan became aware that his wife began showing signs of needing to rest from the saddle. "Luke, find a place for camp. We're ready to stop now."

Humph, they didn't last nearly as long as I'd hoped. We still got two hours of daylight. I'll need to push 'em harder tomorrow. The little woman ain't gonna be much help in me getting' 'em wore out, Luke thought.

Within the next few minutes, Luke saw the place where he could watch from a vantage point above where he would set them up for camp. Dismounting, Luke took the animals and led them to their space. He removed the packs and threw everything on the ground near where Ryan was busy gathering sticks for a fire. The little wife was busy constructing a lean-to! *A lean-to!* A bower for them to bed in... surprising both men by her expertise. Luke had been watching Millicent the entire way and figured she was just another stupid woman, and and not much of a woman at that. *Hell, she sure is a piece of work. Sorry bitch. Bet the money Mister Trenton is a totin' that she ain't no virgin. Wow! Now that's an idea. When the time is ripe for me to make my move, maybe I'll just have a piece of that before I set off.* Laughing silently he continued setting up the campsite and locating exactly where he'd bed down.

•   •   •

Millicent was determined to make herself as useful as possible and would do her dead-level best to see to Ryan's comfort. Their discomfort and embarrassment regarding their new roles soon gave way to the duties surrounding their mutual needs.

"I've checked out that area over there," said Ryan, indicating a grassy place beyond a small thicket, "for our bodily needs. Use the right side for bladder relief and the far back for bowel evacuation." No way did Ryan suppose this trip was going to be comfortable, but this close proximity to a wife was nigh on to impossible. But, for her sake, he'd need to bed beside her. There's where the itchy part would begin for them both. Having been with Pakuma just last night was fresh in Ryan's memory and easily conjured up the passion shared between them.

Ryan had never been one for bedding the women available at every port they docked. But allowing himself to be pulled into such a perfect union with Pakuma left his mind continually reaching back in to relive those scenes. Shaking his head to clear it of the thoughts, he walked over to where Millicent was weaving in a limber twig and said, "Millicent, really you need not go to such trouble. We'll just ride off and leave it in the morning."

Stopping to look at her husband, she replied, "I know that Ryan, but this is my wedding night and I don't want Mister Newburn to suspect that we are not fulfilling our marital obligations. Particularly on this—our first night together!" Pausing only long enough to adjust the last sheaf of leaves into the overhang, she said, "Now where is our necessary located, again?"

He stooped enough to get to her eye level and pointed toward the thicket.

Blushing prettily, Millicent asked, "Have you already used it?"

"No, I thought you might want to go first."

Rising, she said, "I shall. Thank you."

Ryan watched with good humor as she stiffly made her way beyond the thicket.

Having watched and heard the exchange between his two companions, Wishbone thought, *Stupid fools. I'll go where the hell I want to go. Ain't gonna go traipsing off like some sissy to do my pee.*

• • •

Later, after they had eaten the biscuits and ham slices packed by Wauna, Millicent said, "I find that I'm very thirsty, Ryan. Do we have water?"

With no spoken word, he handed the canteen over to her once he'd removed the top. She drank long and deeply. *I'm gonna need to find fresh water soon and make sure all the skins are kept filled,* Ryan thought.

"Luke, next time, when it gets close to where we'll be needing to camp, see if you can't find us a place near running water."

Damn! What's that stupid fool expect? Then, expanding on that thought, *Yeah, that'll give me plenty of reason to keep 'em in the saddle and get 'em really worn out!* His thoughts had him wearing a veritable grin.

The trio ate in silence and as they sat, staring into the glowing embers of the dying fire, Luke finally spoke. "Headin' up the hill a ways.

Y'all sleep good now. I'll rest lightly and keep an eye open for anything what might want to disturb us. G'night."

"Thank you, Luke. It's very comforting having you with us and taking care to see we get to our destination. See you at first light."

Crawling beneath the shallow bower, Millicent began to remove her clothes. "Don't take your clothes off, dear. You'll freeze to death… and you never know what emergency might arise in the night! In such a wild situation as we are now in, we can never let down our guard for a moment."

With a silent huff, Millicent lay on the blanket and pulled the loose side over her prone body. *I won't get an ounce of sleep on this night! My wedding night!* Within five minutes both men could hear her snores.

Ryan lay listening to Luke moving around the perimeter. Luke prided himself on his self-taught ability to move unseen and unheard. He simply had no idea that Ryan knew his every move, and one might even venture so far as to say Ryan could almost read his thoughts. Being an Indian had it benefits.

•   •   •

The sun was high and the small party was well underway across unchartered territory. The men knew they had the possibility of coming across tribes, possibly hostile, that they would have to deal with. The day passed uneventfully until Millicent began to complain of hunger and the need to walk and rest her body.

Having filled all the canteens earlier when they'd crossed a nicely-flowing little rocky stream precluded their need to find water where they'd camp down for the night.

So much for that idea, thought Luke

• • •

Upon departing Coloma, the party had gone southwest down the American River, toward San Francisco. About halfway there, they turned due south to meet the Sacramento River. From there they traveled southeast all the way to Fort Yuma. The dense forest had given way to scrub oaks and cacti with mesquite and rattlesnakes, not to mention the furry tarantulas, scorpions, and the rather poisonous Gila monsters.

Millicent suffered terribly in the heat, and her companions did not fare much better. However, before the party left the Sacramento basin, Ryan had thrown away Millicent's frilly clothes and had her dressed in loosely-woven attire he'd gotten from Wauna. With moccasins upon her feet and a bonnet to replace her straw hat, she began to complain less. Ryan had to admit that she had become more pliable, but still displayed the heated looks of desire every evening as they sought sleep. Ryan was finding it more and more difficult to fend off her silent pleas. His own needs were pressing upon him. *Lord, give me strength to hold myself in check.*

• • •

By the time they approached Fort Yuma, they were well-seasoned to the realities and harshness of travel through hostile territory. Upon entering the confines of the military enclave, they were greeted by the commander and given opportunity to rest and refresh themselves. But upon being revived, while seated at the commander's dinner table, they were all plied with questions as to how they made it through Apache territory. Luke spoke, "We found that padding the hooves of our animals, and foregoing all speech, we attracted no attention."

"How did you communicate?" asked Major Heintzelman.

"We developed hand signals… built no fires. Ate only the dried foods we carried, and either Ryan or myself walked and led the others to sleep in our saddles. We stopped only when we found water." Luke sat, now silent, as if he were still out in the plains. Thinking to himself that they would soon be back out again headed eastward, he once again regretted ever ingratiating himself into this situation. He'd thought this trip would be so lucrative it'd be worth all the discomfort. Coming west with a wagon train had not been nearly as traumatic as this was proving to be. *Maybe I can stay here and scout for the military. To hell with Ryan's money belt!*

"How long before you set out again, friends?" the major asked.

"My wife needs another day or two of rest. I suppose we need to be away within the next 48 hours," answered Ryan. "And I'd like to purchase supplies for the trek, if you have any to spare."

"That'll be according to what you have need of, Sir. What is it you'll be wanting?"

"Salt is the main thing. Dried meat, too, if it's available. We can even use fresh meat and cover it in salt to dry while we're on the trail. We are eating cactus fruits where we find it. As long as we can get to water, we'll be fine," explained Ryan. "Making our next leg to Fort Bliss is going to prove just how strong we've become. Both Luke and I are rather proficient in the use of slings to take down small game." Smiling, he continued, "Saves on ammunition."

"How do you cook the fresh kills?"

"We don't. No fires. We salt it down to draw for a couple days, then wash it off and eat away. It staves off the worst of our hunger. Living strictly off the land is an art, I've found. Of course, having our guide with his extensive expertise is really a life-saver. I don't know what my wife and I would do without him."

Ryan was astute enough to know that Luke displayed, albeit unknowingly, his simmering rebellion. By openly complementing his prowess, Ryan was giving him enough rope to hang himself. "Luke tells us that anyone can survive if you know where to find sustenance."

Reading Luke's evident pride by his body language, Ryan knew it'd soon be the man's downfall.

"Well, sirs, and ma'am, I'll have you taken to the quarters that have been prepared for you, and I pray you all rest and sleep well. Reveille sounds at five. Breakfast in the mess hall at five thirty. You may eat then, as there'll be nothing else served until noon." Rising, he bowed slightly, and strode toward the door. "Sergeant, see to it these folks are shown to their quarters."

• • •

Millicent was ill-prepared to mount her horse that morning two days later. She'd found sleeping on a cotton-stuffed mattress far superior to the saddle. Dreading the coming days, she bade the commander and those standing farewell as she rode through the gates with a tremulous smile and a stiff spine. Ryan knew her thoughts, and she rose ever higher in his estimation of her resolve. He just may have to capitulate to her desires.

They had made the first five hundred miles of the trip to Fort Yuma in twenty one days, three weeks from the day they left Coloma. Ryan approximated their arrival to their next break to be about the same length of time. Another three weeks or so to Fort Bliss.

Luke constantly kept to his plans to abandon the party and head off "to greener pastures". This sort of work was not to his liking. Too dangerous. Too many savages to his way of thinking. But he grudgingly had to hand it to the man; Ryan surely did know all about the sneaky ways to survive in this hellacious land of snakes and scorpions. Luke had learned a lot and felt sure he could make it on his own. *I'll head back to Yuma. I kinda liked the looks of that place. I'm sure they'd hire me on in some capacity.*

Chapter XIV

W aking from a sound and restful sleep, Ryan was surprised to find himself in deep darkness. Millicent was snuffling gently by his side. *What woke me?* Remaining still for a few seconds, his senses were on high alert. Then came a gentle nickering from a horse. The *"humph"* of someone settling into a saddle. Quick as a flash of lightening, Ryan was out of his covers and stealthily-silently approaching the corral where the animals were tied. The night was as black as he'd ever experienced. However, that fact worked both ways. Whoever was mounted was as unable to see well as Ryan could. Reaching for the long leather whip that hung on a limb at the edge of the corral, Ryan unfurled it without sound. Then aiming high toward the sound where the movement had been, he cracked the whip into the air with all his strength.

A terrible scream lit the night. Ryan heard the violent curses as Luke was brought to ground in a blast of crushing bags and weapons landing with him. Like the strike of a rattler, Ryan had Luke by the throat, dragging him over to the tree by the corral. Using his whip he bound the hapless man and stood back.

"What's going on, Ryan? What was all that noise? It woke me up." Millicent came forth from their bower bed.

From the dark silence, Ryan spoke, "Go back to sleep. It was just the restless horses."

Ryan sat in front of Luke until the sun began to rise and they eyed each other. "I see you were all packed and ready to leave us with nothing but the clothes on our backs, Luke. I do hope you can understand exactly what this means." Ryan's voice was deadly, and Luke could feel his blood run cold. He had sadly underestimated Mr. Trenton. Without any doubt, Luke had more than met his match.

"Now, Ryan, let's not get hasty. Think this thing out. You need me. Don't tell me you don't. Why else would you've hired me on? I've kept up my end of the bargain. Haven't I?" Realizing immediately his mistake, he began to alter his thoughts. "I mean, I've done everything you asked of me, haven't I?"

"Yeah, Luke, and so much more from the look of things. I need to tell you a little story so you won't be expecting too much sympathy from me." Ryan continued to talk for the next fifteen minutes to his guide, telling in low and gentle words how he had dealt with four men that were thieves and murderers. Watching Luke's face draw into itself in thoughtful horror, Ryan knew he'd begun to give this thief some very good idea of what his fate could easily be. "Now, tell me, Luke, what would you do if you were in my situation? Would you prefer to die right now, or would you like to be given a chance to be rescued?" Silence. "Let's opt for the rescue, shall we? I don't want to upset my wife by killing you out here. It might make her afraid of me, and I wouldn't want our marriage to begin on such a dire note." Silence. "Okay, that leaves us with the chance of someone rescuing you. I guess you know what that means. Like those four gentlemen left tied to those trees… Anyone could have found them and rescued them. Take heart, Luke. Your chances of rescue are infinitely better out here."

Ryan stood and cleaned up the mess left on the ground where Luke had been jerked from the horse. He unsaddled the beast and returned it to the corral. Sorting through the packages and weapons, Ryan called to Millicent. "Wake up, wife, I need your help here."

She was by his side in a thrice. "What do you need, husband?"

"Sort through and repack everything so we can break camp and head out. We'll eat on the trail."

"Why is Luke tied up, Ryan? What happened?"

"That's not for you to worry about, dear. He just got a little rambunctious earlier and had to be restrained. He's alright. I'll take care of everything. Here, let me help you with that. Do you need to relieve yourself before we get underway?"

●　　●　　●

Looking back over her shoulder at Luke tied to his saddle with hands bound behind his back, Millicent knew to keep quiet. Whatever he'd done, she was sure he deserved his punishment. Ryan was fair if he was anything. She shook her hair and smiled into the morning sun as she chewed the salty meat. She gave not one concern about the fact that Luke was not given anything to eat. Well, he couldn't, could he? He was firmly tied. So there!

Several hours later, Ryan stopped by a rapidly-flowing stream. He dismounted as the horses drank. Walking over to Luke, he unceremoniously pulled him to the ground, opened a canteen, and gave him a long drink. Stoppering the skin, Ryan hung it on the horn of his saddle. Millicent had dismounted and gone into a small ravine to take care of her bodily needs. While she was busy, Ryan helped Luke to stand and walked him back up the draw, out of sight from where the horses were standing. Finding a willow with downward drooping limbs, Ryan sat Luke at the base and bound him hand and foot and chest.

"Ain't you gonna leave me with a knife or food or something? At least leave me with my gun."

"I'm leaving you with exactly what you were going to leave for me and my wife. Nothing. You sure won't be needin' the money you stole from me either. Now, I don't want to hear your beggin' as we leave here. Open your mouth!"

"*No! Awhaagg!*" Ryan shoved a wad of leather into Luke's mouth as Luke was trying to shut it, not quite fast enough. Ryan kept stuffing the cavity until he could see Luke beginning to panic. *That's enough.* Satisfied, Ryan returned to the horses just as Millicent emerged from the bushes. He helped her to her saddle, and he tied the reins of Luke's horse to his. The mule and other steed were well-watered and ready for the trail onward.

"Where is Mister Wishbone, Ryan?" Millicent asked.

"He had other plans, dear."

"Why do we have his horse?"

"He really didn't need one for the time being. Now, don't worry about him. He'll fare just fine."

• • •

They made Fort Bliss in three and a half weeks. Ryan did not want to punish Millicent by pushing any harder toward their goal. She was content now with Luke gone. She had never said anything to her husband about him, but she was always uncomfortable with the way Luke leered at her when Ryan's back was turned.

Arriving at the fort, they were greeted by the commander, Lieutenant Colonel E. B. Alexander, and his family. Millicent was royally entertained by the woman, and their stay there was luxurious in Millicent's estimation. Food! Real food. A clean bed! A chamber pot! A wash tub! She almost felt like a woman again. Only the clothes she was wearing kept her from feeling feminine once more. Her dream was a frilly dress… No, a filmy nightgown and Ryan! That was her dream!

She and Ryan were bid farewell by the garrison. Everyone was standing at attention as the two rode out with their pack of animals. Ryan had been given letters to be taken to their next station, Fort Clark, only four hundred miles away.

• • •

By the time they approached the fort, just three weeks later, both of them were anxious to be inside the protection of the heavy walls. They'd missed an Indian raiding party by the skin of their teeth last evening just at sunset. Ryan had been able to see the fresh tracks where previous parties of Indians had crossed. Being as near to the fort as they were, he determined that this path was nearly under continual use by the Indians to constantly keep the fort under their surveillance. Knowing the natives had a propensity for moving during twilight, he figured they'd better stay put for a while, just in case. If he and Millie had anything on their side, it was time. It simply did not benefit anything to get stirred up and hurry around. One could lose one's scalp by losing one's nerve.

He had made the decision to heed his inner senses. "Quickly, Millie. Dismount. Quietly. Let's get the horses upstream. See, beyond those willows."

She had not been unaware of the close calls they'd had in their travels, and she obeyed Ryan without the blink of an eye.

He had pulled himself and Millie to situate the horses and mule facing away from the crossing area downstream. They were camouflaged by the downward sway of the willows. They had stood facing their animals, holding their faces close and stroking their muzzles to keep them from making any sound. Adding to their cover was the fact that sight was greatly diminished during the gloaming hour. They stood unnoticed as the small war party quickly made its way across the shallow stream and continued without any hesitation.

Ryan had held them still and silent for half an hour more before he relaxed enough to take a deep breath. Leaning over to his wife, he whispered, "I believe we can mount up now. Do you need to take a break before we leave here?"

"I don't think I can, now. Maybe later when we find our camp for the night."

He was always on the alert as to where he spied previous activity and steered clear of those areas. His keen senses had kept them safe. He considered that his years with his Miwok family had certainly given him a heightened intelligence of Indian ways, which came in good stead during this long trek through hostile territory.

•   •   •

Ryan was greeted by H. A. Hamner, and he produced the letters from Fort Bliss. Later, after supper, Ryan was called into the commander's office for a brandy and some conversation. Curiosity was the commander's reason, he had said, but Ryan knew better. He immediately was forthcoming with everything he had gleaned of the activity of the Apache's, through whose territory he had safely come. "I'd like to offer you the job of scout for this garrison, son. You and your little wife would find comfortable quarters here. What do you say? I believe I can even get you a commission and rank to compensate you for your troubles."

Smiling at his host, Ryan shook his head. "This country doesn't have enough money to entice me away from the goals I've set for myself and Millicent. You see, I've plans to hit the Carolinas before I begin to slow down. My desire to know my new country is greatly pressing upon my heart, and I find that God has blessed me with the wherewithal to accomplish that desire... But, I do sincerely appreciate your offer, and if circumstances were different, your offer would be well received. As it is, my wife and I shall be on our way within two days. To tarry longer would not benefit our determination to push on while our bodies are in top shape for this strenuous travel."

"Certainly, I can understand your view, and honor it. You, sir, are a rare individual. I perceive you shall attain your every goal in life. I envy you your youth and drive. But, here, let us finish the evening with a tad more brandy and one of these fine cigars."

"Thank you. But, no thanks. I do not care for smokes, nor at this juncture do I need to dull my senses with that fine brandy. I'll hold off on such wonderful vices until later when they can be better appreciated. I'll bid you good evening, if I may?"

"By all means, young man. See to your rest. Breakfast is served at seven sharp. No doubt you shall be awakened by the bugle."

•   •   •

Back on the trail, Millicent was dreaming of the time when she could live like the wife of Commander Hamner. Her clothes were so beautiful and she was so gracious. Millicent just needed to be given the chance. She'd show Ryan what a wonderful, dutiful wife she could be.

Simultaneously, Ryan was panting for New Orleans. He expected to find some serious and lucrative business ventures to attach himself to there. Just six hundred more miles. That would surely cost them a month at least. Probably more, as Ryan could see his wife was—in spite of her bravado—breaking some little bit at a time. She had become less ebullient. Her smiles became more forced. Her attentiveness to him strained. At that moment, Ryan made the determination that this night he would consummate their marriage.

Breaking for camp near a clear stream, he saw, with hidden satisfaction, Millicent religiously constructing the protective bower for their bed. Every night, without fail, if there were the necessary materials available, she made their nest. During the prairie crossing, she had to be content to shelter them beneath sagebrush or mesquite. Sometimes, she'd push cacti over to catch another and spread the tumbling weeds around it, nearly making a private room. He smiled knowingly with thoughts of their first love making.

Ryan suggested, after they'd eaten, that they take the opportunity to bathe somewhat in the cool waters flowing nearby. She was thrilled, as he'd never allowed her to take the time. He always insisted she be dressed in case of an arising emergency. The only real baths she'd had were at the forts they visited. Stripping quickly without embarrassment, she stepped into the chilling water and with indrawn breath she plunged deeply beneath the wonderful, head-clearing bath. Within a few seconds she was taken by surprise as Ryan grabbed her body and pulled her into his embrace. His lips sought and found hers. With happy abandon, she threw her arms around his neck and squealed in delight.

With his hands, he gently rubbed her body and stroked the water through her hair as she lay back to his ministrations. Ryan had become very engorged by then, and he held Millicent as he lifted her from the icy water to carry her dripping wet into the bower. As he laid her upon the warm blanket, he said, "Dear wife. Tonight I make you mine. Tonight I give myself to you. You truly are a most unusual and strong girl. Yes, you are still a girl in age, but in sense and strength, you are far beyond your years. Millicent, I will love you. I promise from my core being, that I shall do everything in my power to keep you safe, to care for your life and your happiness. To have you never fear for my commitment as it shall always belong to you alone."

"Oh, Ryan. You've made me happier than I thought I could ever be. I love you with all my heart."

He lay gently beside his young wife and became her lover. The glory of it all was so intense she began to cry. "Oh my God. Have I hurt you?" Ryan asked.

"Never, husband. I'm crying from happiness. I had given up thinking this would ever happen. I cannot believe God has blessed me so with such a wonderful man. I love you so much, Ryan. I promise now to do everything I can to make you happy and to help you realize your every dream."

Between kisses and snuggly whispers, he said, "Are you up to us trying it again?"

And the bower rocked.

• • •

The lights of New Orleans could be seen shimmering in the distance. Ryan and Millicent were so excited to finally arrive. Making camp for the last night, they would enter the city tomorrow before noon. Their bed this night lay beneath moss-hung oaks, while the animals munched the sweet green grasses within their corral.

New Orleans was a thriving, bustling city, full of business dealings. Exactly where Ryan wanted to be. They followed their noses to a wrought iron-embraced hotel. Ryan and Millicent entered the cool interior to find dark men and women dressed in crisp white clothing. The women had turbans wrapped around their heads and the men were busy polishing crystal chandeliers and brass fixtures everywhere. "Do you know where the proprietor is?" asked Ryan.

"Yes sir. Step this way, please, sir." Ryan and Millicent followed the young man out of that room and on into another, this one carpeted and dressed with large palms along the walls. Chairs and couches and ornate tables were scattered across the space. A few strangers were seated hither and yon behind newspapers, and hardly rustled their papers to take a peek as to who had entered.

From behind a marble-topped counter, a rather rotund man said, "May I help you, sir, ma'am?"

"Yes, please. We need to obtain a room for several days. And depending on our plans being fulfilled, we may be here several months… And I'll need to find the closest livery to house our animals."

"By all means. Will you please sign here? I'll have Peter bring in your belongings." As the man snapped his fingers, a young lad came running to the counter. "That really won't be necessary. We have it all right on us. The only thing I really need is for the animals to be taken care of. If Peter will take these bags and lead my wife to our room, I'll see to the horses."

"Yes! Here, Jack. Come help this gentleman find his way to Charlie's Livery and bring him back straightway."

Within half an hour Ryan was back and entering the room assigned to him and Millicent. They were both relieved to be, at long last, in decent surroundings outside of the military camps they'd visited.

Next morning, after a sumptuous breakfast, Ryan spoke to the man at the desk. "Sir, my wife and I need your help in obtaining a wardrobe of clothes befitting our stay in your city. As you have easily ascertained, we came from a great distance and wore only the attire fitting for horseback travel. We, both of us, need new clothes. Do you have any suggestions as to where we might avail ourselves of such?"

The man reached out his plump hand, which Ryan took and shook. "Let me introduce myself. I'm Barron LeClerc." He continued, "Not royalty, no. My Creole mother thought the name would stand me in good stead. She said 'Barron' will always be honored... Anyway, I have good friends, a husband and wife who are a tailor and dressmaker. Their business may be found just three streets away, and I'll be more than happy for Peter to take you there at your convenience."

"As soon as my wife is ready, I'll let you know. Thank you, LeClerc."

•   •   •

Some three hours later, Millicent and Ryan left the establishment after having all their measurements taken, patterns selected, and fabrics chosen. Monsieur and Madame Fontaine assured their new clients that one suit for the gentleman and one day dress for his lady would be ready for delivery before the evening meal the following day. Until then, Ryan and Millicent stayed close to their hotel, but Ryan gleaned much information from LeClerc concerning the important contacts he must make while in New Orleans. He was anxious to get it accomplished and be on his way toward Mobile. He expected, that if all went as he hoped it would, he should finish with all the contracts within a month, two at the most. Also, all the finery they'd ordered from the Fontaines should be ready by then. Ryan and Millicent bought new trunks and cases in which to store all the new clothes. They planned to be riding coach to Mobile, giving them both a well-needed rest from the saddle. The livery had, indeed, already bought their animals, except for one horse which Ryan kept, Whistler. Where Ryan went, Whistler went. It was uncanny how Whistler could read his master's mind. They were as one, mind and spirit.

The weeks advanced and the weather became hotter and stifling. A miasma seemed to settle on the city, and Ryan noticed many personal coaches, packed to capacity, leaving for parts unknown. Still, he was able to connect and contract with a classmate of Paul Robertson, lawyer Kenneth Byrnes. Ryan produced letters of introduction, thereby alleviating many questions about his ability to hold up his end of any agreement. Also, letters from his banker in San Francisco, and from Carl in the land office, stating that he had verified the existence of the lode in the cave. Carl had been awarded 10% of the gold, with 40% given to Frank and 10% into an account set up for Pakuma. The rest was being deposited into Ryan's accounts at Brannan's. There was very little hesitation on the part of any business he approached. Ryan bought into the Picayune, steam ship lines, the fledgling railroad, the breeders of strong horses for carrying mail, the ports, and even pried one ship's captain out of trouble and filled the hold with timber for California. Ryan's fingers had the Midas touch, and his contacts soon began suggesting others who could benefit together with his backing. Consequently, he bought into the import company bringing French wine to America. A brandy distiller showed up one afternoon as he and Millicent were at supper. Within an hour, Lawyer Kenneth had been summoned and a deal was made forthwith.

They had been in New Orleans about two months and Ryan had informed LeClerc that he'd purchased passage on the stage set to depart two days hence. Millicent excused herself. "I don't feel at all well, dear. I cannot finish my supper. I must get up to bed before I will not be able to."

Ryan jumped up, excused himself from the men at his table, and took his wife's arm. Helping her up the stairs, he noticed she was a little hot. Once in the room, he helped her undress and into her gown. As he was trying to get it over her head, she leaned forward and vomited.

Quickly wetting a towel, he wiped her face and laid her back onto the bed, pulling the sheet over her nude form. Going to the door, he called, "LeClerc! Send a maid up now! My wife is ill... and send for a doctor."

Half an hour later, with Ryan still by her side, Millicent began to rally. The doctor had been in to see her and pronounced that she was simply suffering from the throes of early pregnancy.

"My darling, I do hope you're as thrilled as I am over this wonderful turn of events! This bit of news lifts my spirits to the highest! Beyond what I ever considered they could be. Why, Millie, you've given me greater joy than any man ought to ever expect from this side of heaven!" He leaned over to lay gentle kisses over her smiling face. *A family. A real family. My own family. Thank you God.*

"You've made me so happy, husband. You've fulfilled my every desire. I love you so..." But as her eyes began to close, she continued, "I feel somewhat tired... sleep... " She drifted off.

Ryan rose from the bed and went over to comb his hair and straighten his attire. Going to the bell pull, he summoned a maid. Standing at the opened door, he waited until he saw her coming up the hall.

With a small curtsey, the girl said, "I'm Gretchen, here to see about your wife."

"Stay nearby. My wife is sleeping now, and I find I must leave for an hour or so. See to her for me. If she wakes, simply explain to her that I should be back before ten."

"Yes sir, I will. You can count on me. Monsieur LeClerc has given orders to the entire staff that your and your wife's needs are to be met at any cost." Again, she did a small curtsey and closed the door to the darkening chamber.

After fifteen minutes or so, Gretchen had seen no movement from the high, testered-bed, so she decided then would be her best opportunity to hie off to the kitchens for a quick supper. Slipping quickly down the stairs and off around them toward the back hall, she ran toward the merchant's entrance and on through the double set of doors into the hot kitchens. Grabbing up a heavy china plate, she helped herself to a dip here and a chunk there and a biscuit, before setting forth to the dining hall beyond the heat of the activity.

•   •   •

Ma! What are you doin' here? We all thought you were gone! Where is the baby? How long have you been back? Have you seen Pa?

Millie tossed and to and fro in the damp linens of their bed. She could feel her mother's arms enfolding her trembling body.

Why, there's the baby. He's so pretty. What does Pa think? I'd love to see him. Do you know that he and the boys are working in my husband's gold mine? Did I say, 'my husband?' Yes, Ma, I'm married now. The doctor told Ryan that I'm pregnant. Isn't that something? Here I'm giving you your first grandchild just a few short months after you've given me a baby brother. They can grow up together. Uncle and nephew. But, right now, I gotta go, Ma. I gotta go…

•   •   •

Gretchen rose from her chair as Ryan entered the candle-lit chamber. "How is she?"

"Been sleepin' away. She hasn't moved this whole last hour, sir. I've been right here, watching. No movement, nor anything."

Ryan reached into his change pocket to lift out a small gold coin to lay into the palm of the young girl. "You may leave us, and I thank you for your attendance upon my wife."

She bobbed a short curtsey and swept out the door.

Ryan undressed quickly and slipped on his night dress. Regarding his sleeping wife, resting peacefully in the center of the bed, he removed the night clothes and redressed in the attire he'd just removed, deciding he'd rest better fully dressed, if he had to sleep on the settee at the foot of the bed. After a few moments, he rearranged the furniture to accommodate his tall frame and tried to settle down. Finally, giving up, he found another comforter in the top of the chiffonnier, which he threw on the floor. Laying his body upon half of it, he pulled the other over his form and had no trouble finding a deep sleep.

A hefty prod against his left leg awoke Ryan immediately. Sitting erect, no one was there. He knew something had awakened him. Throwing off the comforter, he stood to see his wife still deeply asleep, although somewhat pale. Thankful that she was getting some well-need rest, he quietly tread, barefoot, over to the side of the bed. Laying his hand upon her breast, he found she was no longer breathing.

The cook downstairs in the kitchen was the first to hear the high keening cry of Ryan Alexander Trenton as he fought against the surety of something over which he had no control. His Millie was gone.

•   •   •

LeClerc had the Doctor sent for, who brought with him Monsieur Boussard, the mortician. Ryan was beside himself with the bursting horror of being out of control. His mind warned him that he was no better than anyone else who'd suffered like events. Why, think of Millie's own father Frank... losing two sons, a new baby, and his wife too! Frank's life was going on. But Frank had been thrown a life-line. Who would throw him one? Who was there? No one. He was once more alone in this world. All the riches he had amassed could not hold a candle to Millicent, his beautiful Millie.

Ryan had been led by LeClerc down the steps and off into the small dining room, away from the back stairs, seating him at a table well away from the activity soon to take place when the body of the beautiful Mistress Trenton would be taken out of the hotel via the rear entrance. Her death needed to be kept quiet as long as possible.

Panic over the untimely deaths occurring with far too great a frequency could easily begin. No need to stir up the masses.

A hefty portion of whiskey was dispensed by Clyde, the bar tender, for both gentlemen. He poured one for himself and drank it down quickly, then poured another. He himself had lost his two eldest children two years back from this very malady. Here it was again! They called it the yellow fever, and few recuperated from it. Very few.

With tremendous foresight, LeClerc set to having new quarters opened for Mr. Trenton, and all of his belongings moved there. He also directed Lucy and Junie to pack all the Missus's clothes and personal articles into cases to be set aside until told what would become of them.

As the day progressed, Ryan sat in a stupor, until a Reverend Tidwell came and sat with him. "Sir, please let me introduce myself. I'm Albert

Tidwell… the shepherd of the flock of Saint Michaels over on Barrow Street. I've come to offer my help with anything you might need."

Focusing his eyes on this new interloper, Ryan spoke, "I appreciate your trouble, sir, but I'm in no mood for help right now. Just leave me be… let me mourn the loss of my bride. Anything that I want to have accomplished concerning my wife, I will speak to LeClerc and to Attorney Byrnes. I do believe they will be able to provide for my wishes to be fulfilled." Rising, Ryan spoke again. "I bid you good day."

He remained standing until the reverend rose and left the room. He then asked the bartender where LeClerc had gotten off to. "I do believe he's seeing to your new quarters, Sir."

"New quarters?"

"Yes sir. The maids will be cleaning your old room, and so they will put you into another for the time being, sir."

Turning, Ryan said, "Yes. I see. Well, I'm going to head out to see if I can find Mr. Byrnes. I think I just might need his help."

•   •   •

That evening, Ryan was in the unenviable position of writing a long letter to Frank, explaining exactly how he'd lost his daughter. Ryan tried to open his heart enough to expose his emotions to lend some credence as to the deepness of his sorrow over the loss of Millie. He wrote page after page, tore and crumpled page after page, until finally he'd decided to be satisfied with the words he was presently reading. They left so much unsaid and unexplained. Ryan new he'd never be happy again, never fall in love again. There was only one Millicent. His family was gone.

He steeled himself to accept the hand dealt, and was completely assured that he'd never again commit to anyone. He was so torn asunder by the loss of this first love, until he found it impossible to even breathe deeply. His mind told him that his life before her had been shallow and filled only with the pursuit of wealth. His riches never caused him pain. He enjoyed the emotional aloofness afforded by the inanimate wealth

And freedom it gave in providing him the ease to accomplish whatever he desired.

Never again would he allow himself to become attached to another, but he knew he would seek and find a woman to take to wife to provide children to inherit his vast fortunes. He wanted to establish a dynasty: the Trenton Dynasty.

At the grave site, Monsieur Boussard laid into Ryan's hand a small silk bag which contained the gold band he'd removed from the hand of Madame Trenton. "I had my daughter, Diane, make this for you. My wife used to make the little silk bags, but she, too, has been taken by this malady."

Ryan clasped Boussard's hand in simple "thanks," and slipped the bag into the fob pocket where he kept a supply of small gold coins along with his gold watch.

After Millie's burial, Ryan completed, over the course of the next three months, many more lucrative contracts. All during the weeks, he witnessed many deaths occurring throughout New Orleans. The dirges were heard daily. Everywhere he looked were mourners. The city was emptying out rapidly. Coaches fully loaded were seen rumbling out toward wherever the people could feel safe. The city had begun to burn barrels of tar, hoping to waylay the spread of the disease.

Ryan went about whatever business he could contract. Many times he had to forgo meetings with appointments already made because the person was either out of town, or in mourning over the loss of a family member, or else having succumbed to the malady themselves. And being in the throes of mourning his personal loss gave Ryan a laissez faire attitude. He performed everything within a shell of unreality.

"LeClerc, I've come to settle my bill and to bid you farewell. Too, tell Lucy and Junie that they may take anything of the possessions that belonged to my wife. I will be leaving as soon as Charlie gets here with Whistler. Your kindness and understanding are much appreciated." Ryan reached to shake hands and said, "See that my letter is posted to Mistress Trenton's father as soon as the carrier comes through. It's very important."

128

Chapter XV

The weather was still very warm, but one could tell the seasons were changing. September had passed and October had opened with its relief of milder temperatures. Arriving in Mobile, Ryan was never so glad to finally arrive at a destination. Pushing himself as well as the faithful Whistler, they had arrived at last to the point where they could both take advantage of well-earned, much-needed rest and recuperation.

First off, Whistler was housed and cared for in a nearby livery owned by a beautiful woman, Maria Montparssant. Ryan was impressed with her expertise in providing for Whistler, and with her assurance to himself that her charges were reasonable.

He queried her as to the best hotel available, but still not too far distant from the livery. He was directed to Hotel De Ville not fifteen minutes' walk from where they stood. She called Jimmy Chu forward into their presence and said, "Get the cart, Jimmy, and port this fine gentleman's possessions along to the De Ville, please."

Ryan's long strides kept the diminutive Jimmy in a veritable trot as they made their way across and down the well-packed streets, arriving quickly at their destination. Entering the sumptuous establishment, Ryan strode immediately to the long, beautifully polished marble counter, behind which stood the stately desk clerk. "Might I help you, sir?"

Completely unaware of the deep scrutiny of himself by the clerk, Ryan said, "Yes. I need a room for several weeks, please."

With great effusiveness and apologies Ryan was met with the sorrowful shaking of the clerk's head. "Sir, please, forgive us, but we find ourselves in a terrible quandary. At this moment in time most of our rooms are already filled and those vacant are not nearly up to the standard expected by a gentleman such as yourself. I so deeply apologize." Drawing himself up somewhat, he continued, "However, sir, I have the answer to your needs. I shall see to your greatest comfort in the fine home of the Matron of Mobile. You see, sir, whenever our establishment finds us in this untenable situation, we have a beautiful understanding with the lady. Her home, known as the DuBois House, is located very near. I shall see you taken safely there via coach, if you will accept our offer, sir."

Unhappily disappointed, Ryan met this snag with typical stoicism. "Fine, but I'll take my horse instead. I want him kept where I am. Does this home have a proper stable?"

"Of that you can rest assured, sir. Here, Jimmy, run back and fetch this gentleman's steed." The man continued, "Sir, if you'll just follow me I'll see to your supper and a bit of rest while Jimmy takes care of everything. He'll have your horse ready and packed by the time you finish your meal, which is furnished gratis. And, before that, let me take you to the W.C. close by where you may take care of your needs and lave a little before sitting for supper."

Ryan was led into a back hall through the door leading into a small but elegantly furnished wash room, where he relieved his bladder into a wall unit which was flushed from the tank of water posted high upon the wall. Turning, he found a large porcelain bowl filled with fresh warm water, with fine milled French soap (Millie's favorite) and a stack of pristine linens. Making quick use of the facilities, he was met by a large— very large—black man upon exiting back into the hall. The man motioned to Ryan, who silently followed. Led into a quiet dining salon, the aproned waiter met him and took him to a small table near the front windows.

"Might I suggest hearty fare for a travelling man?"

"That would meet my needs verily. But, might I have a glass of red Bordeaux, and a bit of bread to prepare my taste while the foods are being prepared?"

Bowing and backing away a few feet, the waiter motioned to a pretty young lady, and within a minute or so she brought forth a cut crystal glass and a dusty bottle of wine. The maître d' came immediately to wipe the bottle and show the label to Ryan. He then pulled forth the cork with a snap, and poured a bit off onto a napkin and then a swirl into the waiting glass.

Ryan watched the heavy wine coat the inner side of his glass and then brought it to his nose to sniff deeply. This was fine wine. He looked at his server and simply nodded. The wine was lovingly dispensed into the glass, while the pretty young lady laid a small basket of warm bread onto the table near Ryan's elbow. They both left him free to ken his situation with grateful appreciation of their kindnesses, and then to humbly reach inward for the deep sorrow that Millie was unable to be with him on this adventure.

•　•　•

Two hours later Ryan found himself astride Whistler, trotting in the light rain behind "BigUn," the huge black man appointed to lead him to the DuBois House. They made an amusing picture: Black BigUn clothed in stark white, astride a small black mule. Ryan, bringing up the rear, could only see the white clothing ahead and nothing else. The scene was as if a massive ghost was showing the way to the unknown world of angels. Only, thankfully, angels wore white?

Periodically, the full moon would find its way between clouds to display the surrounding flora. Ryan pressed on behind the apparition ahead of him. Before too long, the guide pulled up and turned to call to Ryan. "Hit's right up this line of trees, suh. Just you keep straight ahead, and the house'll show herself. You won't have no trouble, suh. They'll know you be on the lane well afore you actual gits there. They'll know."

Without further word, BigUn turned and rode toward Ryan, who put his hand out and stopped his guide. Reaching into his vest pocket, Ryan drew forth a small gold coin which he placed into the hand of BigUn. "No sir, you don't need to do that, sir. I be well taken care of by the hotel."

"Yes, take it and get something for your wife, with my thanks."

With a huge grin displaying his white teeth, BigUn said, "I be indebted to you, and the wife I'm gonna git soon will too." With those promises, the men went separate directions.

The drizzling rain had stopped, but one could hear the heavy drops slipping from the leaves as Ryan moved on down the lane. Sure enough, before long, he spied the large white house shimmering in the moonlight like an opal. The shadows cast by the moving clouds made the facade appear a living thing. As he drew closer he became aware of the rustling magnolia leaves and the air was scented with the dying cones of the blossoms. Breathing deeply, he once more realized his body was healing from the horror and loss. He sat taller in the saddle and took in the sight and subdued sounds of the enveloping night.

Tethering Whistler to a black iron post set into the lawn about thirty feet from the front steps, he lifted his valise and walked up the broad stairs onto the wide porch, which he crossed in six strides. Lifting the lion's head knocker, he rapped it loudly, four sharp strokes. Almost immediately, he saw through the leaded glass of the door, the glow of a lamp emerging from inside the house and coming forward, toward him. He backed up a few steps as the door was swung inward.

The first thing seen by Ryan was a shock of wild white hair. The elderly black man stepped forward, reaching down to lift the valise, as he ushered Ryan into a large central hall. Placing the valise at Ryan's feet, he said, "I'll see to your horse and the rest of your luggage, sir. Come, I'll have you wait in more comfort, sir. The lady shall be with you shortly." The very proper English spoken by "White Hair" was not lost on Ryan.

Ryan took the opportunity to survey what was able to be seen from where he stood. Aware that the central hall rose, unhindered by floors or walls, for two stories. The curved stair was free standing and turned back over itself in a large spiral. A sparkling crystal chandelier hung suspended from a dome, high above the lower floor. He supposed one would be forced to stand upon the stairs in order to light the many candles. *How in tarnation do they change them?*

Standing in the center of the floor was a tall, round table holding a large Chinese vase filled with a plethora of blossoms which permeated the air with heady perfume. *I could have provided this for Millicent.*

Bringing the guest's attention back to the here-and-now, the deep resonant voice from White Hair spoke, "My name is Absalom, sir, and I'll fetch my mistress. You come with me for now."

Ryan was led off to the right side of the rotunda into a wide hall, and as the first door was opened, he was led into a comfortable room with shelves lining three walls, all filled with books. A library or office of sorts. Lighting several candles, Absalom said, "Make yourself comfortable. There's brandy over on that chest, if you desire."

Ryan deferred taking a seat as his clothes were still somewhat damp from having come through the light rain. Making himself at home, he strode around the large room, regarding the several portraits hung on the walls between the windows as well as over the ornate fireplace. Appreciating the china figurines and heavily-decorated Chinese vases, he finally poured himself a small amount of brandy in a large snifter. He was deep in thought, gazing into the face of the portrait of a young priest, when he heard the rustle of silk fabric behind him. Turning, he actually caught his breath for an indiscernible moment as a most beautiful young woman came toward him with hand outstretched. Her long dark hair was caught back with a deep maroon silk bow which matched her gown. She was about the same age as his Millie, maybe a year or two older.

"Welcome to the DuBois House, Sir."

Ryan took her hand, bowed, and brushed his lips ever so lightly across the back. He raised up. "My pleasure to meet you Madam Claudette."

"Oh, no, sir." She smiled. "Claudette is my grandmother and owns this house." She continued, "I am Katherine DuBois, the only child of her deceased son, Alphonse. But, please, sir, how can we be of service to you?"

Ryan explained that the clerk of the Hotel DeVille had suggested the DuBois House would provide accommodations while he was to be in Mobile on business.

"How long do you expect to be in this area, Mister—Mister..." she hesitated.

Quickly he stammered out his name, "Ryan, ma'am. Ryan Alexander Trenton. I will probably be here a month, maybe longer. I've business to conduct in Mobile, as well as taking a much-needed rest before leaving for the East. Would this pose any problem for DuBois House?"

"No, indeed, sir. Grand Maman will be thrilled to have you here for as long as you care to stay." Turning to leave the room, she bade him sit comfortably to finish his brandy while she made sure his horse and any other baggage he might have was taken care of. "Shortly, Absalom will see you to your room. I do hope you enjoy your stay with us and that you will have your needed rest while here. I bid you goodnight."

"Thank you, ma'am, and a good night to you." Ryan sought out the leather upholstered desk chair, knowing the dampness of his clothes would bring about no harm to it. Seating himself, he sighed and sipped the burning brandy. Soon, he set the empty snifter aside and rose, once more to regard the beautifully appointed chamber. Anxious for Absalom to return, he began to pace. Turning, he saw the door open and Absalom motioned for Ryan to follow him.

"Sir, your horse is well taken care of and your luggage is awaiting your arrival in the room that has been prepared for you. If you'll come with me..."

Without further ado, Ryan quietly allowed himself to be led back into the wide hall, only to turn right and continue on down the deeply-carpeted way toward a tall window glistening from moonlight filtering onto his path. At the end of the hall, Absalom opened a door on their left, which revealed wide, accommodating stairs leading straight up toward the next floor. He opened the upper door, which led into a wide hall identical to the one below. Here, they turned left and headed toward the central rotunda seen in the distance.

Standing aside, Absalom opened the second door on the right wall, and ushered the guest into the room, already alight with candles. Ryan was impressed with the chamber. "Your luggage has been opened and everything sorted and laid in the drawers of the highboy. The two suits have been hung in the next room where the steam from your bath will aid to release the wrinkles. The staff will be available to launder any clothing and return it ironed and folded. Boots left outside the door will be polished and replaced before you arise in the mornings."

"Absalom... Absalom, is it? I very much appreciate the great care of the DuBois House. I can only regret my wife is not here with me to enjoy it. She would have loved being here."

"Thank you, sir. After your bath, a small treat of foods will be brought up to assuage any bedtime hunger. Too, there's an assortment of spirits, or you may request something else, such as tea or coffee. We are at your service, Master Trenton."

After Absalom left, Ryan began to undress as he headed to the small room just beyond the massive headboard of the high testered-bed. He heard the large copper tub being filled and was looking forward to a long-refreshing bath.

"Evenin', sir. I'm Tobias, and I'm to help you with your bath."

"I thank you, Tobias. Let's get to it." Stepping gingerly into the steaming water, Ryan found that, even though it was hot, it was not so that he could not appreciate it. Laying back into the curve of the tub, he closed his eyes as the young man soaped his head, massaged his shoulders, and he scrubbed his tired back. "Mr. Trenton! Wake up, Sir! We don't need you to drown. You hurry now and finish up before it's too cool. Here's the towel, I'll bring your bed shirt."

Ryan dried quickly and donned the loose, comfortable cotton shirt that fell below his knees. He had no house slippers, but Tobias located a clean pair of socks to protect his feet from the cool tiles in the bathroom.

Returning to his bedroom, Ryan spied a silver platter resting on a table in front of a freshly-lit fire. Lifting the lid revealed a chunk of yellow cheese, a perfect pear, three hefty slices of warm bread, and a crystal carafe of white wine. Ryan had literally been all over the world, but never had he been met with more graciousness and care than was being given at DuBois House.

While taking the refreshment, he considered his surroundings more fully. The walls of his room were covered in coral-colored silk. The large highboy was wrought in gleaming mahogany and stood like some stiff sentry against the wall near the door. Upon the floor lay a rug of oriental design, mostly in white or cream wool, featuring a corner design of several twisted limbs laden with coral-colored blossoms, while the rest of the rug displayed a scattering of the blossoms as if they'd been blown off the limbs to nestle helter-skelter. To each side of the open fireplace stood two high-backed wing chairs upholstered deep gray silk, each with matching foot stools. Beyond the right side of the bed stood a black lacquered screen imbedded with mother of pearl accents which formed a stunning oriental scene.

Having eaten his fill, and now with glass in hand, he walked over to the double windows to draw open the heavy drapes. The windows revealed twinkling lights several miles away. Ryan supposed it might just be Mobile Bay. Seeing his bed already turned down and ready, he set the wine glass back on the tray, and opened the windows to the chill of the night air. Smiling, he snuffed the candles and crawled beneath the deep covers and hardly knew he was prone.

• • •

Sunlight streamed into the chamber, but Ryan's face was burrowed deeply into the embroidered pillow cases, snuffling gently. Young Tobias spoke before he dared touch the guest. "Sir. Sir! You're bound to be hungry! Breakfast is bein' served and the lady of this house is anxious to meet you. Sir!"

Rolling over, Ryan asked, "What is the time?"

"It's beyond eight, Sir. Mos' everybody done eat and gone, but Missus Claudette is waitin' to meet you. You been asleep nigh on to ten hours, sir. You want I should help you to git dressed?"

"Just show me the chamber pot, and you can go."

"S'over behind the screen. I've brung yo hot water to shave. It's in the bathroom a'waitin'. I'll run tell Missus Claudette you be on yor way a' bien tot."

Ryan found the relief he needed behind the screen and then into the bathroom to clean his teeth, wash his face, and shave. Dressing as quickly as possible, he entered the hall. Turning toward the rotunda, he sped in that direction. Bounding down the circular stair, he stood, momentarily unsure of where to find the breakfast room. Materializing from nowhere, Absalom said, "Through the doors there, sir."

"Thank you, Absalom." Stopping momentarily to gaze around the open rotunda, and then up at the glittering crystals of the unlit chandelier, he asked, "How in blue blazes do they get all those candles lit?"

With a few steps off toward the back wall, Absalom opened a door so disguised as to be unseen by an uninitiated eye. Walking over to see what Absalom was disclosing, Ryan was enthralled by the view of a series of pulleys and chains, and watched in fascination as Absalom grasped a chain and released a lever. "Watch the chandelier now, sir."

As smoothly and silently as the morning sunrise, the chandelier was lowered until it was almost touching the flowers held within the vase. "What we do, sir, is move the table and lay down an old sheet on the floor. The girls clean off the old wax and polish the crystals before putting in the fresh candles."

"Ingenious! That's what it is! Who in the world came up with this idea, anyway?"

"Why, Mistress Claudette's nephew, Father Speterrie. His portrait is over the fireplace in the library."

"Oh, yes. A fine looking young man. Thank you. Now lead me on to the dining room, or wherever the breakfast is served."

"This way, sir. We'll take the route through the loggia so you can enjoy the atrium."

Before opening the door at the far end of the loggia, Ryan spied a very large parrot eyeing him maliciously. "Gold and money! Gold and money!"

"Does he say that no matter who passes?"

"No, indeed, sir. His vocabulary is extensive, and we've found him to be foolproof in his assessment of most everyone." Absalom smiled broadly.

"Humph! He's liable to have his neck wrung by exposing what he shouldn't."

"What intelligent person would ever put stock in what a bird says?"

"Right you are. I'm being paranoid, I suppose."

Standing at the closed door, Ryan could hear voices of several people in animated conversations. He drew open the door and entered a beautifully appointed room, not large but very sufficient for its purpose. The men, two of them, stood immediately. "Please, take your seats, sirs. Allow me to introduce myself. I am Ryan Trenton, late of California."

"California? Where is that?" inquired one of the gentlemen.

"The newest territory, sir. Won by America fighting against Mexican forces. And have you not heard how gold was found in abundance in that new territory? Why, from what I saw, half the East was abandoned and headed there for the opportunity to find their fortunes."

"Yes, I do recall something about that, now. And why did you leave there, sir?"

"If you don't mind, I'd rather not discuss my decisions with folks I've just met," countered Ryan with an ingratiating smile.

"My sincerest apologies, sir."

An elderly woman spoke up. "Do come in, and find yourself a seat here, near me at the head of this table, sir." Then, she looked toward the young man standing attendance at her elbow. "Tobias, call Mary in. Viet, Viet!" Then, back to Ryan, she said, "You have the pleasure of my company now, as have I, yours!" She cackled, and to Ryan she resembled for all the world a veritable "Jolly Roger" image!

Mary, a stunning young mulatto girl, hied to her mistress's side and curtseyed slightly. "Yes, ma'am."

"Fix a generous platter for our latest guest, Mary. Please." Smiling genuinely into the sweet face of her servant, Claudette nodded toward the sumptuously filled sideboard. "Now, sir. Let me introduce you to our present guests who are as anxious as myself to interrogate you." Laughing, she continued, "We were all aware of your arrival yester' evening, and you have been given the last of the rooms available here at DuBois House. My other guests have been here somewhere between one week and one month. But more about that later. Quickly, now." Motioning to the two couples, she began, "Monsieur et Madame Fletcher, Morgan and Anna. They are here from Georgia." Smiling, she continued, "On an extended honeymoon, I believe."

Ryan stood and bowed toward the handsome couple, reached across to shake Fletcher's hand, nodding to Anna, and then regaining his seat.

"And this," indicating the other much older couple, "is Monsieur Lester Aymes and his lovely wife, Beatrix. Both from New Orleans and in search of safer quarters... and there we have it. As soon as you've finished your petit de'juner, we'll retire to the east salon, if you will allow it, sir."

"Thank you, ma'am. I'll be more than pleased to spend some restful time in good conversation with you fine folks. I find myself ready to give over to lethargy for some little while to recuperate from too much trauma, the details of which I shall reveal." Upon finishing most of the foods on his plate, he rose to take his cup to the sideboard to refill with the strong, black coffee from a large silver urn. He returned to the table, where he lifted a biscuit from his plate and said, "Shall we depart to the east salon?"

Hurrying to her side, the ever-present Tobias took Madame Claudette's frail arm at her left side, opposite from her cane, to steady her as he lead her toward a set of curtained French doors. He gently flung them both wide into the salon, and in so doing, caused the sheer curtains gathered over a wall of windows along the east side to billow inward by the vacuum. The room was sparse of furniture. A floor of Spanish tiles was covered within three feet of the walls by a turkey carpet of dense wool patterned mostly in maroons and blacks. The brown wicker seating pieces were pulled toward a low, marble-topped table of gilded wood. Large floor pillows of tapestry scenes were stacked, after a fashion, over in a back corner. Taking up the most space were columns of varied heights topped with squat porcelain planters filled with greenery. Ryan recognized the ferns, but most of the other plants he could not identify.

"Open the curtains, Toby, please."

As Tobias did so, Ryan realized that the windows were really four sets of double doors leading onto an expansive patio. From where he could see, it appeared the patio was several feet above the gardens beyond. *There must be steps, I'd say at least four, to the path below.*

Even though the room was situated eastward, it maintained the cool of the night simply by the shade of massive, moss-hung oaks. Meandering throughout the gardens were brick pathways where one could obtain closer views of the assorted plants there. *Millie would have loved ...*

"I perceive your mind is far away, my friend. Would you care to share with this company your deep thoughts?"

Once more, Ryan turned his mind toward the room of companions. Regarding the mistress of this house, he likened her unto a rusty pirate who wore all her booty for safekeeping. Madam DuBois was tiny, brown, and wrinkled. He surmised her to be one hundred if a day. Drenched in diamonds, from a multi-strand collar around her scrawny neck, to several odd bracelets on her left wrist, where she kept shoving them upward toward her elbow, he supposed to prevent them slipping off her claw-like hand. Not every finger held rings, but more did than didn't. Her earlobes were stretched long by the large, pear-shaped diamonds swinging from them.

Severe black. Every inch of her outer clothing was black. The bodice was of softest lace over a shiny, black under blouse, and the bustled skirt was of a silk taffeta, which rustled nicely as she moved. He never spied her shoes, but assumed them to be high-buttoned boots well-fitted. Probably handmade locally.

The elder couple was dressed in simple, inexpensive clothing. Well-worn footwear. No jewelry outside a gold watch, the chain of which was seen across his dark vest, and a plain gold band on the missus's left hand. A very unassuming couple. His kind of people, if anyone cared to know.

The Morgan's were, to his mind, easily taken. Mister Morgan was observed peering anxiously at Ryan more than once. Ryan was certain the man had kept his wife from her planned excursion so he could pry out as much about Ryan as possible. Maybe he had a scam planned if he found Ryan to be gullible. *He's met more than his match. This may be entertaining.*

"Your silence, sir, has us all with bated breath."

Shaking his head a little, "Clearing the cobwebs of sleep, ma'am. Forgive me, but there's really not much to tell. I am a man alone, taking my time to travel on toward the east of this country. I have hopes to purchase a bit of property someday and build a home, somewhat on the order of this edifice."

"No small dream," Fletcher Morgan spoke up. "You evidently have the purse to accomplish this?"

"Let us hope so, sir," Ryan answered in clipped tones.

"Share with us why you have not found a wife to accompany your life."

"Why? Do you have one in mind, ma'am?" Ryan was becoming a bit testy by the perceived inquisition.

"Forgive our ineptitude, sir. Please. I do confess that you were the subject of conversation before you came down for breakfast. The other guests had left for previous commitments, or they too might have stayed. I fear my curiosity is infectious. You see, sir, you are here because of my intervention. I have a standing request for the manager of Hotel De Ville to send anyone out here to DuBois House if he thinks I might enjoy knowing them."

"Do you mean, ma'am, that there may possibly have been a chamber vacant there, but because he deemed me as being interesting to you that I was denied a place to rest?" Ryan spoke with force.

"Oh, please, sir. Do not become agitated. I'm doing very badly in attempting to allay your unrest in this situation. No harm was meant.

141

Ever. Only the whims of an old woman were trying to be met. You see, my last husband built that hotel, as well as provided most of the funds to the banks to allow for the building of Mobile. The name of DuBois is well recognized hereabouts, and consequently—as long as I'm alive— well revered. I humbly beg your forgiveness for your understandable concerns, however unfounded they are."

"I see. Well, for a few moments I felt as though I had been led as a lamb to the slaughter. As soon as I can again see my way clear before me, I'll begin to share myself. Until then, how about you all doing me that same courtesy?"

With this unexpected turn, Madam Claudette cackled loudly. "He's turned the tables on us all! I see you are a man of superior intelligence, and one well worth knowing... Here now, you, Fletcher Morgan, give us all your story. "

Literally backing his head onto his shoulders, he said, "I have no story! Let Anna speak." Turning to his young wife, she glared at him as though he'd sprouted horns. Taking this opportunity to gouge back, she said, "I met Fletcher in a barn on my daddy's place. He was hiding from—he said—an irate father whose only daughter he'd been betrothed to, but left at the altar. The incident was quite a while back, but the father and his daughter have long memories. My daddy gave Fletcher his oldest nag and saddle and five dollars and told him to get out of the country that night."

Fletcher had slunk down into his chair as deep as possible, with face aflame, as his "sweet Anna" continued unabated with the tale. "Now me, being fifteen and full of piss and vinegar, decided I must leave with him. He is, after all, rather handsome, don't you think?" Looking askance at Fletcher, she continued. "I told him to wait for me, that I'd be right back with food. Hah! I packed a small valise with a few clothes, and threw in a few biscuits and a bottle of wine that was on the kitchen table, and fled out the door to the barn. Daddy had already gone back to the house by the side garden, so there was nothing to stop me. I made Fletcher saddle my pony and we rode out that night. We've been together now for about six months. Never married, but I call myself Morgan to save face."

Flinging her curls, she smiled and finally looked at her husband, *unh*, her lover.

Laughing raucously, the five rocked back and forth, slapping knees and wiping tears. At last, Fletcher gave up and joined the laughter, as did Anna. Ryan began to realize he was on the way to full healing, and of all the people to deliver that healing! At that point, Ryan made up his mind that he'd do what he could to mentor the young man into an honest and lucrative life, as soon as he returned Anna back to her family. They must be frantic. After all their daughter was only fifteen and would need their blessing for a marriage to take place.

"After we've heard from the Aymes, we expect you, Mister Trenton, to be amenable to sharing some of your life. Agreed?"

Feeling much relieved at the situation, he nodded.

"Alright. Now for our next entertainment, albeit I cannot imagine it will surpass the wondrous story of Anna's, let us hear from your corner, Mister Aymes."

"Oh, I fear ours is very uninteresting. You see, Beatrix and I have been together fifty-two years. God allowed us to enjoy our lives as neighbors, growing up together, falling in love as youngsters, and being given the blessings of our parents to marry. She came to live with my family right away as I, an only son, took up the reins of my dying father. From that point on my mother gave up and literally wasted away. Within two years, Beatrix, at the age of seventeen, became the matron of our home. We never had children. Well, that's not exactly factual." He glanced over at his wife who sat silently with eyes downcast. "We lost every one of our babies before it was time. The yard behind our house holds the graves of seven. Finally, we quit trying to have children. It was the most difficult thing to do. Our love for each other made it difficult for us to remain apart. But in deference to her health, we kept to ourselves in that way. I know this is probably more than any of you wanted to know... certainly more than you need, but it's so much a part of our struggles through these years until now at this age, we've become lovers once more and God has given us peace and joy to carry us forward to our graves."

Silence. Tears. Sorrow for literal strangers. Each one looking into their own heart to commiserate spiritually with this wonderful couple. Gleaning so much from their courage. Comparing their own experiences with those of strangers, Ryan could see why Madam DuBois so needed this interaction with the myriad of people being forwarded into her life by a caring individual. Living vicariously, intertwined within the lives of strangers provided a balm to one's own traumas of life. *Every person has a story to tell. Yes, Ryan, every person is a gift.*

Inch by inch, Ryan began to open, heart and mind, as these individuals related portions of their lives. What a treat it was. Certainly something he'd remember all of his life.

"In order that we might allow our newest guest a bit more time to gather himself, I shall give you the abbreviated story of myself." Settling anew into the well-pillowed wicker rocker, Madam DuBois glanced at each person individually, that they may feel totally included. "I was born Claudette Ghent in the small port of La Rochelle, France. Growing up near the sea gave me the ideal opportunity to meet many wonderful seamen. The three men that I was privileged to marry were all wealthy sea captains. Their fortunes, one could say, were won by ways many could consider to be somewhat clandestine. But, during those times, piracy wasn't frowned upon. Nor is it very, even now. As navy was pitted against navy, ship against ship, the bounty gleaned was divided amongst the crew. My last husband built this home for me in this direct spot so I could watch for his return home from the sea. From the widow's walk atop this house, the port is easily seen. Possibly you, Monsieur Trenton, have an excellent view from the windows in your room?"

Ryan nodded. "Yes, Ma'am."

"Back to my story… The first husband was lost at sea hardly before I'd learned my new name. Then my second beloved was killed in hand-to-hand combat when boarding a captured vessel. The ink had barely dried upon our marriage contract. My last husband was Emile DuBois. We had one child… a son that we named Alphonse. Emile and Alphonse had left Mobile and gone back to France to retrieve Emilee, Alphonse's wife, and their baby daughter Katherine. As his ship entered the gulf here, a storm of unprecedented strength tore it apart upon the turbulent seas. All aboard were lost. Except..."

Here she paused for effect. "Absalom and Katherine. They ended up clinging to a wooden door. He kept the baby girl fast upon that pitching door by tying her, using his shirt, to the knob. He held her for nigh on to a week. They were circled by sharks. He was stung by jellyfish. Sunburned beyond belief. Not one ounce of water or food to sustain them. But prayer. Absalom kept his prayers rising day and night. At last the storm abated and he saw sails of fishermen in the distance. Nearly overcome with fear that they would not see them, he prayed harder. Suddenly there were water birds circling over them. Gulls, pelicans, albatrosses. They would fly toward the fishing fleet and then back out to where Absalom held our precious Katherine. When they were finally taken aboard a boat, the men feared Katherine was dead. Absalom told them that she was not, but only asleep. She would awake during the violent storm, smile sweetly into Absalom's worried eyes, then lie back down and drift off to sleep once more. Absalom told this as fact. He knew God had kept them both safe."

Reaching for a cup of tea that had been silently brought into the room and settled upon the low table, Claudette continued. "Once the fishing boat brought them to shore and found out exactly what had transpired, the townspeople began to speak of Katherine and Absalom as 'the miracles of the storm.' To this day the older population of Mobile still remember and speak of those two in those same terms. My love for my family is now totally tied up in one dear child. Katherine will inherit everything I own. And there's more than one sees here." She swept her hand about, as her guests were mesmerized by the glitter of all the jewels she wore. "What you do not see are the many domestic and foreign holdings from the husbands I was so privileged to have. Each man loved me enough that their initial business was to see to my care if anything were to happen to them." Sipping the hot tea, she looked directly to Ryan. "I do believe we've given you ample opportunity to gather your thoughts for our edification. If you please?"

"Well, I fear my life shall provide little in the way of entertainment for you, but... To begin with, I was an orphan. I had neither mother nor father to know. I do wish I had some idea of the kind of people they had been. But that just isn't to be."

Smiling, Madame Claudette said, "Sir, I perceive your parents were beautiful people. Why, just look at you... tall, physically fit, thoughtful gray eyes, and a full head of hair a most comely shade of golden brown. You are indeed a very handsome man."

Ryan, somewhat embarrassed, glanced over at young Anna, who was blushing prettily while clinging to the arm of her husband-to-be.

"But, do continue. Don't allow my interruption to stop this story. I must know of your adventures."

"As I was saying, I was born in London and completely unable to care for myself until a wonderful woman, Abigail Cavendish, found me starving in an alley behind their kitchen. She literally saved my hide, and her husband—one fine man—owned a tap room and restaurant, and had several rooms upstairs for travelers to rest overnight. I was put to work there. By the time I was around eleven years old, I was taken by Captain Confidence Witherspoon of the trading ship, *Narcissus*. He taught me all there was to learn of the sea and sailing. By the time I was around twenty-one or so, we landed in New York harbor and loaded the ship with supplies for California."

"What route did you take to get there?" asked Claudette.

"Why, we went around Cape Horn. A long and arduous journey, and my captain was on death's bed at the time. I had been recently promoted to first mate and had command of the ship during that part of the journey. Needless to say, we did make it to San Francisco. There is where my life took a turn into a completely different direction." Ryan hesitated. "Mind if I have a sip of tea? My throat seems to be dry at the telling of this tale."

"By all means, sir, sip away." Smiling with genuine pleasure, Claudette was literally clapping her hands in anticipation as she watched him pour and stir in a spoon of sugar.

"Now, where was I? Oh, yes. In San Francisco. There I was kidnapped and held prisoner. Since I was rescued before the miscreants could finish their plans for me, I became deeply indebted to my savior-as-it-were—a Miwok Indian girl by the name of Pakuma. The rest of the story is somewhat unbelievable as I married the daughter of newly-arrived immigrant, Frank Martin. When his eldest daughter found out I planned to return east, she literally begged to go with me. Since she was still but a girl, we decided it would serve us better if we were able to present ourselves as husband and wife. So we were wed. We had every intention of living a platonic marriage. So as soon as I got her back to Carolina to her family there, we expected to have our marriage annulled. However, the best laid plans of mice and men, you know. We entered New Orleans in July past, and she contracted yellow fever and died. She's buried in a church yard there."

Claudette caught the "platonic" relationship and the "best laid plans" part immediately. "Did you consummate your marriage to this girl?"

"Do you really want to know that?"

"It isn't necessary, no, but if there hadn't been more, I don't believe you'd have spoken those particular words."

"You're correct. Millie was pregnant when she died. I lost wife and child in one fell swoop. I'm hoping this trip on toward Carolina will help me to heal, and all the while, I'm planning on making several business contracts while here in Mobile. And, indeed, in every major city I find myself in."

The six friends settled back to cogitate the aspects of the different lives they'd become privy to. Ryan's eyes wandered outside to catch a glimpse of Katherine walking with the beautiful mulatto girl, as they cut and gathered blossoms to fill a large trug. As the sun crept higher into the faultless sky, he could hear the cicadas begin their whirring sounds of short-lived joy. He was wonder-filled with the knowledge of her miraculous salvation of life upon a door. Absalom was surely kept in high esteem by the old woman, having been gifted with the last of her family by his fortitude and prayers. Ryan watched as the two turned back toward the house, walking slowly-arm in arm, before they turned toward the west side of the house and disappeared from sight. A feeling of abject disappointment stirred itself into Ryan's psyche.

Turning his attention back to his amiable companions, Ryan rose as both couples stood. "Thank you for a most enjoyable few moments here. Beatrix and I are out for a walk. We expect to be out nearly all day, but shall be back in plenty of time to dress for the supper meal. Is that alright?"

"By all means. Enjoy your time together. We look forward to seeing you later on."

"Anna and I are doing the same. Only we will use the rig. I've a business meeting at the bank of Mobile later this morning. We too, shall be back for supper."

Everyone had left the salon except Ryan and Madame Claudette. He bowed over the extended hand of his hostess and whispered, "Do you need me to contract any business on your behalf while I'm in the city? You may trust my honesty as well as my discretion."

"Yes, I know, Ryan. Presently there is nothing I need you to do for me, but I thank you for your offer." *I am just waiting for you to prove yourself a bit more... I have plans for your life whether or not you believe it. As Absalom kept God's attention on Katherine, I've had His attention on my plans for my granddaughter. She will never marry until I, and God, are ready. He is preparing you for something special. I've yet to be privy to His plans, but I know they are crucial.* "I bid you au'revoir." Turning, she reached toward the seemingly ever-present young man. "Here, Tobias, come and help me to my chamber."

Chapter XVI

A t the stables, Ryan had Whistler saddled, and he rode out the long lane and on toward the route directly into the city. In his solitude, he considered the unsettling remarks by Madam Claudette. *No one would ever have control over Ryan Alexander Trenton's future. Rest assured!*

Glancing upward toward the sky, Ryan was surprised to watch the sun disappear and dense, roiling clouds plunder their way inland. Within a few minutes, Whistler became skittish, as lightening streaked across the blackness. Immediately, Ryan turned back toward DuBois House and sped in that direction. Leaving Whistler in the capable hands of Mister Crawley, Ryan ran toward the nearest door—that of the kitchen. Bounding up the high steps and onto the wooden porch, he was greeted with happy smiles and welcome smells emanating from the huge fireplaces and stoves. "Come on in, sir. You almos' be wet. Hit's comin' fo sure! We gits some mighty fine storms long this coast. But DuBois House can sho' handle 'em. Don't you worry none. Come on in. You'll fine Miss Katherine right on through yonder." The rotund cook pointed across the open divide toward the loggia.

"Thank you."

Entering the door into the glass-walled area, Ryan watched as Katherine and Mary were moving the aged parrot into an inner room of the mansion. About that time, Tobias led Claudette into the library at the front of the house. "I see you returned before the storm sets in."

"Yes, ma'am. I don't much mind the storms, but my horse became too skittish for me to have enough control, so we came back."

"Well, join me in the library. We'll enjoy a smoke, if you've a mind to."

Katherine came sweeping into the rotunda where Ryan was preparing to enter the library behind Claudette. "Grand Maman! I suppose you've noticed the weather has become somewhat threatening? Mary and I shall prepare the house for this one, I think."

"Yes, dear child. I do believe that may be needful." Turning to reach for Ryan's hand, Claudette said, "Come, sir. Let us enjoy some little while in the library, where we can discuss the weather—among other subjects."

"No, Grand Maman, I'd have him join me and Mary in securing the house. I think he might find it of interest."

"Oh, alright. Then go, sir. You'll much more enjoy the company of my granddaughter."

Katherine looked toward Ryan as he came to her side. "Follow me... Mary, call the others, please."

Ryan could hear Tobias as he called on back through the house, alerting helpers to accomplish this "house-securing" business.

As Ryan entered the loggia once again, he was stunned to see no longer the glass wall to the atrium, but instead the room was battened about with wrought iron fretting enforcing tall boards. The loggia was now as dark as a prison, but lit with candles—enough to light one's way through. Walking on through, into the room where he'd taken breakfast, Ryan discovered it too was dark with the windows tightly shuttered. On into the east salon; there, too, was all secured against whatever forces nature might wield against it. Katherine led him on, entering the rotunda once more to see that it too was presently being encased. Ryan stepped out the front doors and turned to watch as the entire façade was sealed. He imagined Claudette now seated amidst lit candles in the library, enjoying her smokes. Looking upward he saw women at the windows, busily closing the heavy black shutters.

When Ryan again came into the rotunda, he was greeted with the central chandelier fully ablaze with what must have been a hundred candles. Even though the wind had picked up, it could barely be discerned. And so tightly secure was the house that there was barely a waver among the candle flames high above his head. "It looks as though you are going to be seeing firsthand what one of our famous storms looks like. We're well prepared to protect these quarters."

Katherine was ill-assuming Ryan had not encountered much in the way of powerful weather systems. Many more dangerous upon the seas than upon land he'd weathered. He recalled one such violent encounter. Captain Witherspoon had ordered them all rope-tied to the masts to prevent them being swept overboard. But he was amenable to her desire to show him "her storm." So, he followed her silently.

"Come, sir. We shall install Grand Maman into her bedroom where she'll be more inclined to nap comfortably while the house is busy." Entering the dark library, Katherine found Claudette asleep in one of the leather chairs situated in front of the fireplace. A comforting fire was crackling away, the long brown cigarillo had burned out in a heavy crystal ashtray, and a half-consumed brandy sat abandoned upon the leather-topped drum table at her elbow. Motioning for Ryan to get the cane and secure Claudette's right arm while she took the left, she called, "Grand Maman! Wake for me please. We'll be taking you in to your room for a while. You'll have a fire in there and you can rest better on your bed."

Rousing herself enough to aid them in her transfer from the library to her chamber just across the hall, Claudette allowed herself to be taken into her room. Ryan supposed they had long since made her chamber available downstairs to preclude her need to get to the upper floors.

•   •   •

Smiling and reaching for his hand, Katherine asked, "Would you like to really see the storm at her best?"

Ryan answered, "I never knew storms had a 'best side,' but yes, I am willing." He gently chuckled.

"Oh, indeed, yes. Why, Mister Trenton, storms provide so many wonderful elements to our world and hold such tremendous power! I'll enjoy your company. Come."

"Where are we expecting to go in this weather?" He definitely was in no mood to go out. He could now hear the muffled rumble of thunder and the crash of lightening and the howling of the winds as they blew against the stalwart house.

"Not outside. Unless we want to. But come see."

They made their way up the central stairway and off into a wide hall at the left. She opened a door and they mounted a narrow, steep-staired shaft with a door at the top. He could hear the sounds of the storm with even greater force now, and figured they must be heading for the widow's walk.

Setting the candle onto a small ledge before opening the door, Ryan saw they were indeed entering a small enclosure erected onto the roof. It was formed of wrought iron grills set outside the hand-blown glass panes. He could see one was able to walk all the way around on the narrow balcony surrounding the glass-protected room in which they now stood. But even with the protection of the glassed enclosure, one felt vulnerable to the elements raging outside.

Speaking loudly, trying to out-blast the cacophony of sounds around them, he asked, "How often must the panes be replaced up here?"

Katherine laughed with genuine enjoyment and said, "Pretty often, I'm afraid. But I love this part of the house most of all. I'm told I am a miracle of the storm, and I suppose I love storms for that reason. Do you care to come out onto the balcony with me to catch the untamed beauty of it all… without the hindrances of man-made protection?"

Ryan blanched as though she were daft. He did not care to go out, but neither did he care to seem a cowering fool by staying in the relative safety of where he presently stood. Against his better judgment, he heard himself declare, "Of course, I'll go," regretting the words as they left his lips. She slid the door open, and he followed as she stepped out onto the high balcony. She grabbed the skirt of her yellow silk gown and held it tightly. Immediately the wind swept the wide yellow ribbon from her long, dark curls, out into the tallest oaks circling the north side of the house. The wind was whipping her beautiful hair wildly about her head and face. Soon she released her hold on her skirt and leaned against the iron banister into the wind.

By this time the two were on the west side of the enclosure being beaten by large, fierce drops of cold rain. He wondered just how much longer she hoped to remain in such discomfort and danger. His fears were overcome by his fancying how magnificent she was: head thrown back and literally reveling in the drowning torrent. Her thin gown was quite revealing of her body, and Ryan realized the stirring within his own frame. Knowing this must not continue, he reached for her arm to get her attention, and she turned and pulled herself into his embrace and lifted her lips to his. His arms automatically tightened, and she pressed into him. He found himself drowning into her being, totally oblivious to the storm without, as it filled the void within his body. Deepening his kiss, he drew his hands downward onto her buttocks and lifted her to fit more fully upon his manhood. She suddenly broke the spell and stepped backward. "Isn't it marvelous? I mean, storms bring out the joy of living! I absolutely am alive... truly alive when the storms come."

Ryan was of mixed feelings about how little the kiss meant to her. Her expression displayed only joy in the tangle of weather around her. "Katherine, we're soaked to the skin. Shouldn't we be going back in?"

Sighing, nodding, she smiled. "I suppose so. It won't last much longer anyway. I'll soon be requesting that the men remove the protections and get the house back to its normal state. But, truly, I'm sorry you got wet. I do get carried away with my own desires sometimes. But it was so kind of you to join me and I do appreciate it. You know, a joy shared is a joy doubled!"

Ryan was totally astounded by her naivety and openness. He must remember to guard himself from being alone with her too often. Standing within the widow's walk, they tried to squeeze as much water from their clothes as possible before entering the stairs.

•   •   •

Standing at the door of his room, Katherine placed her hand to his chest and said again, "I am truly sorry you got so wet. I hope your clothes aren't ruined. I'll have Mary come get them and see to it they are brushed as they dry. Your shirt and the rest shall be laundered forthwith and returned before this day is out."

"I have been caught in rain before, but never deliberately, I must say. Though, I rather enjoyed the experience and look forward to the next storm." He smiled, and she returned it with a full-fledged grin.

"I'll have water brought, and leave you to your own devices. Will you be down for the noon meal?"

"Yes. I'll go out later if the storm has truly past. I need to get into Mobile."

"Good, I'll see you at dinner, then."

•   •   •

Ryan entered his room and went into the bathroom where he undressed. As he was in the process of shaking out his trousers to assess the damage, Tobias knocked briefly and entered without permission. "Here's the water all ready for you... I see your clothes are all wet! Yes sir! That lady does love a storm, and the bigger the better!"

"Yes, you are right. That adventure is something I never dreamed to do, and I don't ever expect to be caught doing it again." They laughed together.

As Tobias was leaving with the bundle of wet clothes in his arms, he asked, "Do you expect to be here for dinner?"

"Yes, Mistress Katherine has already spoken to me about me about the noon meal. I'll be there. Thank you."

Ryan bathed and dressed in clothes he expected to wear on his business trip in to Mobile that afternoon. Downstairs, he entered the library where he spent the little while left before the noon meal sitting contentedly behind the desk, smoking one of the small brown cigarillos and sipping Bordeaux wine. He was gazing out the front windows when he spied the young couple coming up the drive in the rig, soaked to the skin. What a sight. From his vantage point Ryan could easily see that young Anna was crying and Fletcher's countenance appeared as though cloaked by a dark cloud! Rising, Ryan quickly left the library and headed to the front entrance, calling for Tobias as he entered the rotunda. By the time he reached the front doors, Tobias was at his side. "I'll need you to see the rig to the stables, then meet me at the room of the Morgan's with bath water, please.

Without a blink, Tobias replied, "Yes sir."

"Come in the house. See here, I'll help you two up to your rooms."

"Oh, Mr. Trenton! I've never been so embarrassed! Just as we got to the bank, the bottom fell out and we got so soaked until they didn't want to let us in. I can't blame them! We had nothing to do but come on back," Anna cried.

"Say, this is good of you, sir. I didn't know how amicably we'd be welcomed back here. Especially in our sorry state," apologized Fletcher.

"Never apologize for something over which you have no control, my good man." Ryan was, if nothing else, a most perceptive man when it came to assessing the immediate needs of another.

• • •

At the door of their room, Ryan asked, "Will you two meet me in the library as soon as you've become comfortable? I have a proposal that may interest you."

"By all means, sir. We shall be down shortly. And thank you for your kindness in aiding in our arrival."

•   •   •

Poking his head into the library, Tobias asked, "There anything else you need, Sir?"

"As a matter of fact, yes there is. Would you be able to provide three small wine glasses? And empty this ashtray. It's beginning to become odoriferous." Walking over to the window, Ryan flung open the casement, which flooded the room with dampness, but also welcome fresh air. Within minutes—with the ashtray out of the room—the unpleasant stench dissipated, and Ryan poured a small brandy for celebration.

In what seemed like mere seconds, Tobias was back with a clean and sparkling ashtray in attendance with crystal wine glasses and an unopened bottle of white wine atop a large silver tray. He placed it upon the desk and deftly pulled the cork from the bottle, poured out into the fireplace only enough to rid the wine of any cork shreds, then gently decanted the remainder into a tall-necked bottle. Ryan watched his ministrations with appreciation as to how well this young man had been taught.

"Thank you, my man! Now, if you will please advise your mistress that the Morgans and I are taking a moment here in her library. We shan't be long. We'll be prompt for the noon meal."

Silently nodding, Tobias disappeared.

•   •   •

Twenty minutes before noon the Morgan couple tapped lightly upon the library door. "Come in," Ryan invited.

"We just wanted to make sure you were still waiting for us, sir. We're feeling much better now and so relieved to be in your company. Thank you, once again, for your kindness. Anna here seems to think you some sort of god-of-goodness!" he tittered.

"Would that I were, Fletcher. Please, may I call you Fletcher? And call me Ryan, if you will."

"I'm honored to speak on a first-name basis," replied Fletcher.

"Might I pour wine? Brandy? Do you care to smoke, Fletcher? Mademoiselle?"

Seating themselves before the fire, Ryan set a small table between them, then he pulled the desk chair in close where he faced them both. Reaching to light Fletcher's cigar and one for himself, he then poured a little wine into one glass, handing it to Anna, and tipped a small amount of brandy into two snifters for himself and Fletcher. Sitting back and taking his time, giving the couple time to become attuned to him alone, Ryan spoke. "Fletcher, Anna, I have a proposition for you both. That is, if you want it. You may or may not be desirous of the situation I'll present. If you do not, that is fine. However, I'll do whatever is in my power to aid you two into a lucrative position." He paused. "In order for me to see if there is any way that I can help, I find I must delve somewhat into your lives. Is that alright with you both?"

Both nodding, Fletcher said, "Why, yes! Anna and I are ready to help ourselves with your help."

"Fine. Now, Fletcher, tell me what you are best at doing."

"I've got to admit that I'm ill-suited for a desk job. My life is best spent out-of-doors. Anna has the promise of inheriting some property from an uncle… understanding she is named in his will. Her father's brother—Rudolph Borden—passed away about the time we left together. Word caught up with us, but it was too late. We were heading to the bank in the hopes of borrowing against that inheritance."

"Uhm, I see. For now, let's forget that possibility exists… after all you aren't married yet! But if we can solve your dilemma you'll be better prepared to reap whatever benefit may be derived from his will. But to the present. Do you have any skills of any kind?"

"Sadly, the only thing I was ever really taught was the running of our plantation. Being the second son, I always knew that I didn't have a chance to inherit our place for myself. I was courting the young lady—an only child—of a rich landowner next to the property of Mister Borden. I've got to admit that I was expecting to take over the running of that large plantation owned by my then fiancée—Gloria Byington. Everyone knew her father, Horace, was very ill and not expected to rally. As ashamed as I am to admit this about my intentions, I have to say my conscience got the better of me. Knowing the only reason on earth I was going to marry was so I could have her plantation, I did, indeed, leave Gloria on the day of our wedding." Looking over at Anna, he smiled. "Anna came into my life like a fresh spring breeze." Reaching over to take her hand. "She was... no, *is* so innocent and precious. Brought nothing into our relationship except her desire to be with me. For her sake, I must get myself straightened out and become serious about providing for her." Dropping his shoulders, he gazed at Ryan. "Perhaps you have some hope for me."

"Perhaps I do. We shall see... But, first things first, Fletcher. You and Anna must return to her home. I'll have a letter of introduction of myself, my intentions for you and Anna, as well as your contriteness about absconding with his child—even though she somewhat coerced you into taking her with you. How amenable are you two to doing this?"

"How about telling me the plans you have for me first. Then, I'll let you know if Anna and I feel it's worth our while to walk back into the lion's mouth." He smiled.

Ryan was pleased to see this young man at least had enough sense to reckon with him about his situation.

"Very good. Yes, I propose—once you and Anna are wed in the presence of her parents, and you can present me with proof thereof—to begin a salary. One we shall negotiate. You will be paid regularly to travel a route that we both shall be aware of, toward the lower Carolina. Ultimately I shall purchase land and build a home somewhere in the South. I think I'd like it near the Savannah, if possible. You shall keep in touch with me, and I with you during your sojourn. In the meantime, I shall be travelling alone, stopping where I am able to search for the lady to accompany me as my wife."

"How shall we begin?" Anna asked, looking at her husband-to-be.

"Immediately after dinner we shall seek an appointment with my lawyer here in Mobile."

Tapping upon the door, and then opening it, Tobias informed the trio that they must get themselves to the dining room, as Madam Claudette was anxious to see them.

Chapter XVII

H ave a seat, please. Mister Lambert will be free to confer with you all in just a few moments."

"Thank you, Tollison."

An hour later the trio left the Lawyer's office with everything accomplished to the huge satisfaction of everyone. Ryan was pleased to have a hand in shaping the future of this young couple. Working with the network of attorneys to cover every aspect of this venture, Ryan would be pulling the strings to build the life he had envisioned—that of setting Fletcher and Anna in charge of the plantation he would soon construct. First, though, Ryan desired to find a wife, one to birth the family he deeply desired. A comely lady would be his first choice. A comely-but–sturdy, his needful second choice. He smiled in thought.

•   •   •

A few days later the DuBois House bade goodbye to Anna and Fletcher as they headed back to Albany and Anna's home. Some three days after that, Ryan said his farewells to the company of the DuBois House and rode off to continue the journey into his future. He was well into Georgia when he stopped—by invitation—at the plantation owned by Cletus Bradley. Ryan had been in the law offices of Tower and Mobley when Cletus had overheard a conversation between Ryan and Attorney James Tower. Being interested in Ryan's quest for opportunities for investment, and realizing the man to be moneyed, Cletus hung around until Ryan exited Tower's office. "Sir. Sir. Might I have a word with you please?" Extending his hand toward Ryan, he continued, "Forgive me for my interruption, but I overheard the desires you put forth to our mutual attorney, Mister Tower. And, sir, I just may have at least one answer to your quest. Why don't you allow me to entertain you with my proposal over a pint?"

"And you are...?"

Shaking his hand enthusiastically, "Cletus Bradley, sir... of Horizon Plantation, not six miles from here, sir."

"I'm not one to turn aside from a proposal that might enrich myself to an appreciable degree, so lead on, Mister Bradley."

• • •

Cletus found out, via inquiries to the young ladies that clerked for the lawyers, that the young man was wealthy enough for any man to be desirous of him as a son-in-law. But that still left Cletus needing to know about his background, his family, his manners, his honesty, and his aims in life. Also Cletus could be directly involved in helping Ryan locate good properties he knew to be available in Carolina. These facts prompted him to bring Ryan home and hope he'd tarry long enough to choose a daughter from among those of age.

Gladys had given him girls—nothing but girls! There was a houseful of girls and they were driving him crazy trying to locate suitable gentlemen for them. It was his own fault that Gladys had been kept pregnant nearly every year trying to produce the desired son. So as it was, Cletus had six daughters, all in excellent health, with good teeth, and lovely besides.

Gladys finally had enough and suggested that Cletus find someone more agreeable to handle his sexual needs. She had a bolt installed on her bedroom door and from that point on, Cletus had given up. He just didn't have it in him to go 'a'whorin'. Through it all, he stayed faithful to Gladys even though there were times when he wished he'd had the guts to find a willing lady somewhere. But if he were to decide to go out, he honestly wouldn't know where he would begin.

Bringing home this handsome man was the best idea he'd had in many a day. All the surrounding plantations had eligible men who were either too young, too old, too wild, or already betrothed.

●　　●　　●

Six daughters! Ryan had been invited to stay for as long as he desired. Cletus informed Gladys—in private of course—that he'd brought home their first son-in-law, no less! The parents were thrilled by the prospect of finally getting one of the girls married off, and so Ryan was wined and dined with abandon. Ryan had no compunctions about why he was there. This arrangement suited him very well, him being in total agreement with it.

The girls ranged in age from eleven to eighteen, and when they saw the handsome stranger entering the house with their father, they became more animated than usual. Gladys had her hands full trying to get the group to at least appear to be demure and ladylike. Giggles and snickers could be heard constantly, as they snuck hither and yon to catch glimpses of "the man."

Gladys had begun planning a ball as soon as the cotton was in. It would probably be well into winter before it could be held, as the cotton must be tended to first. The ball would involve three neighboring families: the Preston's, the Rankin's, and the House's, along with the Bradley's. Between these families there were seven girls coming of age. Her own eldest was past due for her debut, but had as yet not been presented. Now was the time.

Cletus had done his homework. He'd had his lawyers doing the tracing for him, and it appeared that Mister Trenton's wealth was vast. The word "gold" was spoken over and over, and also investments into a number of lucrative establishments. Cletus was beside himself with the prospect of this man being a part of his family.

Mama had made all the girls wear their best dresses and had spent hours with Tildy over their coiffeurs. They had not been allowed downstairs until supper time. The word from lower quarters was the "he" had been there for dinner, but they had been given light refreshments and made to nap for most of the afternoon. Mama had told them all— even Lucinda, Phoebe, and Maude, the youngest—that they must be on their best behavior. No sniggering would be tolerated, nor would unseemly glances at their guest.

"Welcome to Horizon, Mister Trenton." Ryan was greeted with deep curtseys from six very pretty girls. They were dressed in their finery and on their best behavior as they looked over this tall, handsome man. Dinah was all aflutter, knowing full well that she was the one for whom he'd been brought home. Daddy had always made it known that she was his favorite. But of course, Melinda and darling Corinne also knew they were their Daddy's favorite, and this wonderful stranger had been brought home expressly for them.

Being the well brought-up young ladies that they were, such an unseemly subject of just which one was the "intended" was never broached. They knew Daddy would see to it that each one of his daughters would be well placed. Many men had come seeking approval to court the girls, but none was ever given even a hint as to their suitability for a Bradley miss.

Ryan bowed in front of each young female, beginning with the youngest, and breathed lightly on the back of each dainty hand as he lifted it to his lips. Young Maude blushed delightfully; redheaded, freckled Phoebe clenched her taffeta skirt in a wad with her free hand; lovely Lucinda watched his every move and fingered a blond curl at her neck; darling Corinne held her breath through the entire procedure and nearly fainted; lovely Melinda stood very still and very erect and gazed directly into his gray eyes with her own of deep blue. She felt the thrill of his lips on her hand all the way to her toes. Then he stepped in front of the beautiful Dinah, she lifted her hand up to his face even before he had begun to bow. So embarrassed, she flamed red and coughed gently to get herself to breathe again. She just hoped to faint so as to get it over with. The building up of the excitement as she watched him come up the line toward her was almost too much to bear! *Why, I'll never be able to face him for serious courting… I'm surely going to die before we even get to the dining room! Will he reach for my arm to escort me in for supper?*

When she pulled out of her emotions enough to glance around, she realized the party had turned and were halfway across the hall. He had Mama's arm while all her sisters were right behind Daddy.

• • •

Mister Trenton was there for two wonderful weeks. Never before were breakfasts and suppers so looked forward to. For some reason, he was usually absent for the dinner meal. But two days before he was scheduled to leave them, he sought Dinah's company and asked if he might take her for a walk. He assured her that he'd gained her father's permission.

Excitedly, Dinah had gone up to change her clothes. At Mama's suggestion, she was gowned in heavy, brown bombazine and Tildy draped a short cape of mohair over her shoulders. The weather was cool and she'd been warned not to get chilled and catch cold. She must stay healthy for the Coming-Out Ball, which was but a few short weeks away.

They strolled across a verdant pasture toward the Flint River that ran through Horizon's boundaries. He carried Dinah's cape, for the sun had become very warm upon them. Heading toward some heavy willows and old oaks which lined the river bank, they sought relief from the heat. Dinah was perspiring profusely as she silently rehearsed her forthcoming complaints to Mama about the bombazine!

Ryan helped her to step down a gently sloping bank. As luck would have it, her boot heel struck a small root and she tumbled into him with such force they both hit the ground. She rolled right into his arms, and just as he decided he'd steal a kiss, a bolt of lightning struck a nearby tree and the sky opened with a veritable deluge. He peered skyward, through the canopy of turbulent leaves overhead, and saw the vision of Katherine—the miracle of the storm—smiling sweetly at him.

All thoughts of courting left him, and he lifted the soaking and muddied girl to her feet. Struggling up the now-slippery, moss-laden bank with grunts and groans, he had to literally bodily pull the sopping girl behind him. When they finally reached the edge of the woods and entered the pastureland once more, the clouds had dissipated and the sun returned with a vengeance. Slogging back across the pasture, Dinah was mortified to see that even the cows lifted their heads to stare at them.

With the warmth of the sun on their wet clothing, they began to steam and were a sad looking pair as they entered the back porch off the kitchen wing. Cookie would have been flogged for her outburst of loud laughter, if Mama—who'd just entered the kitchen—hadn't reacted likewise!

Dinah stomped, dripping and squishing, through the kitchen and out the door, heading for the back stairs and her room. Tildy ran after, waving a towel in her brown hand, crying, "Wait, Miss Dinah! Wait!"

Ryan plopped down on the long bench as Cookie called Peter. "Git in here 'n' hep de masser's guest wid his boots!" Like a flash, Peter materialized from somewhere and grasped the muddy boots and drew them off. A drizzle of dirty water poured forth, and as Ryan glanced over at Gladys Bradley shaking soundlessly with barely-contained mirth, he burst out in gales of laughter, which could be heard all over the house.

Dinah was upstairs praying for death to come swiftly, as her sisters circled her silently. They all knew better than utter one word. Even when they heard the riotous laughter from downstairs.

Ryan couldn't remember when he'd ever laughed so deeply and heartily, nor could he think of a time when he'd enjoyed an afternoon walk as much. He truly hated to disappoint his new friends, but there simply was no way in hell he could marry any of these pretty daughters. One more lightning strike from "the miracle" and he'd be fried to a crisp, and any hapless young lady along with him.

The next day, as he was packing to leave, he wondered if it had not been his imagination which had brought to mind the ravishing Katherine when the unexpected storm had burst upon him and Mistress Dinah. Surely, the occurrence was coincidence and nothing more. But he wasn't taking any chances. Besides, he wasn't ready to tie the knot just yet. He wanted to have his plantation up and running, and then to marry. Until then, he felt he simply couldn't betroth himself to Dinah. Sorry, it could not be Mistress Bradley.

On a happier note, if there were plenty of anything, it was men with marriageable daughters. Not deterred, he'd find the right Carolina lady to bear his children.

Heading directly toward Savannah, he found the roads well-traveled. In his valise were excellent leads for land in any number of locations. He felt he was bound to find something he could build his future upon. A place to house his soul. A home with children… his children… yes, and a wife. Of course, a wife.

Chapter XVIII

As Ryan rode throughout Savannah, he was struck with how beautiful the place was, and everyone he had dealings with thus far was generous and seemed to want to accommodate him. In fact, a young man he met in the hotel had just given him a tip about a large parcel of land just beyond the Savannah River, over in Carolina. Being upriver somewhat gave Ryan a feeling that perhaps the land would be less likely to be swampy. In the morning he'd make it his priority to seek out his new attorney. Upon leaving Albany, James Tower had provided him with the name of a lawyer here in Savannah, Georgia, a Mister Gifford Prendergast. If he lived up to his name, then he'd be a formidable ally in Ryan's upcoming dealings.

• • •

A beautiful young woman seated Ryan in comfort to await the arrival of her employer: Attorney Prendergast. The lady would glance shyly over at the newcomer every so often. Finally, Ryan caught her eye and held. "Do you have any idea about how long before Mister Prendergast will arrive?"

"I'm so sorry, sir. He's usually here well before this time. Something unexpected evidently has arisen to interfere with his schedule. Would you care for me to reschedule your appointment? We can give you an hour later on in the afternoon, if that suits you."

Standing and walking over to her desk, Ryan said, "I suppose that might be best. I do have other pressing errands which could be seen to between now and then. Yes, go ahead and give me an appointment later. Could you make it around five?"

Both stopped to turn toward the door as it was swung open so forcefully that it slammed back against the wall. In strode a gentleman who looked for all the world as if he'd been caught in a whirlwind!

"Irene! Call my wife and tell her to get down here immediately!"

"Yes, sir."

As Irene began to lift her hand toward Ryan—who was standing right in front of the irate lawyer—the man suddenly jerked and caught himself. "Sir. I do apologize. Forgive me. Do we have an appointment?" He glanced at Irene, who nodded. "Yes'sir, this is Mister Ryan Trenton." Motioning to Ryan to follow him, he led the way into his office, and he slammed the door. Hurrying out of his wrinkled jacket, he flung it across the back of his desk chair and motioned for Ryan to be seated. Silently, Ryan watched his new lawyer and wondered just what in tarnation his problem was. Curiosity was digging quite a deep hole into his psyche.

Finally, getting himself somewhat under control, the lawyer stilled and looked directly into Ryan's eyes. "Sir, I presume you've come about selling out? I'll help you any way I can. I don't know what will happen to us, but rest assured, we shall fight to the death! Sir. Fight to the death!"

Ryan felt as though he'd awoken into a dream not his own. "No, sir. But since you've just said what you did, I may very well change my plans. May I be privy to your thoughts concerning why you find yourself so upset?"

"Where have you been? Why, there's talk everywhere of this Nation going to war over our Nigrahs. Our Nigrahs, mind you. Down here we take care of our own. This new administration wants to strip us of our God-given rights to own these people. Without them, we'd be sunk. The entire economy of the South will drop off the face of this earth without their labor and our ability to control them. Of course, Louisa and I only have three. Just enough to aid us in keeping up. But it isn't us I'm concerned about. It's the many plantations hereabouts who would literally die if this isn't stopped!"

He paused, and hollered toward the door, "Irene, bring that fresh bottle of whiskey in here and two tumblers!" Calming somewhat, he continued, "I just heard where 'Our Son'—Brooks' nephew—laid into that northern devil, Senator Charles Sumner. Beat him nigh to death right there in the Senate, he did! All I gotta say, sir, is there better not be any reprisals against Brooks or his nephew for this. After all they're trying to do to the South! Trying to kill us, they are, tryin' to kill us all!"

The door opened silently and Irene came in carrying a tray topped with an unopened bottle of whiskey and two heavy tumblers. "Here, Mister Trenton, let us have a touch of Mister Henry McKenna's Kentucky lightning! Best ever! And hard to come by—if you know what I mean." He laughed as he splashed a generous amount into each glass. Handing one to Ryan, he said, "To our mutual benefit and long friendship."

Sipping, then quickly turning up the glass, Ryan finished off the burning liquid. "Aargh! As good as I've ever had, sir."

"Here, have another drop."

"No, thank you. I'd better maintain my equilibrium. But I appreciate your kindness."

"With our world in such an uproar, and likely not to improve for the time being, I doubt I'm going to prove to be much worth to you in your desire to sell out!"

"I do believe you've jumped to the wrong conclusion, sir. I am, in fact, in quest for land to establish a plantation."

"What? Well, in that case, if that's truly what you have in mind, I suppose with the situation such as it is, now is the propitious hour for the best deals to be had. I know of a large place down in the rice growing section-further down the coast..."

"No, sir. What I have in mind is untouched land where I can begin my plantation from the ground up, so to speak. I thought that with land—and plenty of it—I'd be free to follow my desires."

"Very well, sir. If you need me alone to aid in the location of land, I fear I won't be much help. However, if you deem to allow me to make known to my constituents your needs, I do believe it won't be long before something of interest will be forthcoming."

"Yes, well, I don't think that I'll even need your input concerning the locating of land, as I believe I may already have found the area. Only needs to be seen and walked over and surveyed. If it proves to be worthy, and I decide to purchase the place, I'll need your contracts to be drawn up for the seller and myself. Too, there'll be another family to be included along with myself as having total access to the property. But! I'm getting ahead of myself. What I need from you today is your agreement that you accept me as your patron and your promise to use everything at your disposal to aid my satisfaction toward my desired ends. What do you say, Mister Prendergast?"

With little wasted movement, he rose, extended his hand, and met Ryan's eyes directly with his own deep brown ones. "I hereby bind my will to yours with this handshake, sir."

Leaving the office of his newest lawyer, Ryan bade Miss Irene good day, and as he descended the stairs he was joined by an unknown gentleman.

"Sir, sir! If I may, please. I'd like permission to take a moment of your valuable time and speak to you, if you'll allow it."

Ryan stopped short and glanced at the stranger. "You were in the outer office of Attorney Prendergast just now, weren't you?"

"Yes, sir, I was. I perceived you are new in Savannah and could possibly use some knowledgeable soul to help you find your way hereabouts. I'm presently seeking work and would be a worthy hire."

"And your name is…?" Ryan asked, extending his hand toward the stranger.

"Dill, sir. Bennie John Dill. And I'll not disappoint you."

"Alright Dill, I'll give you a go." Shaking hands, Ryan said, "My name is Ryan Trenton, and you call me Ryan, please."

Assuming the descent of the stairs, they crossed the loggia and exited the doors onto the sunny walkway.

"Can you begin immediately, Dill?"

"Absolutely. I'm at your service. And thank you, Ryan, I promise you won't be disappointed."

"I hope not. We shall see. Come. We've got things to accomplish before this day's out. Let's head to the livery to get my horse and one for you. You do ride?"

"Oh, yes'sir! I do ride!"

• • •

Mister Mobley, of the Law Offices of Towers and Mobley, had graciously provided him with the papers of a particularly large acreage of land in the location where Ryan believed his investment would return the most benefit for himself and the Morgan couple. With Mister Dill by his side, the two men rode upland, following the Savannah on the South Carolina side. By mid-afternoon they'd reached a tributary which, from the map, indicated the very easternmost edge of the sought acreage. There was an abundance of wood as well as water aplenty. The land was more flat than hilly, with good drainage. Turning northward, they rode to where an Indian trail was making its way through an open field. This was supposed to be the northern most edge of the property. So far it was very worthy.

The men stopped to rest and allow their horses to graze the plentiful forage. After satisfying their thirst with spring water, with which they'd filled their canteens, they remounted and began riding the westerly leg of the property. Sometime later they figured they'd gone far enough to now locate the landmark for this edge. Seeking a large rock, described as being "flat as a smoothing iron but large as a dog cart," they dismounted and swept through the sparse woods and dry leaves. With sunset nearly upon them, they decided to make camp where they were.

The men cleared enough area for a small fire to be safely lit, whereby they could enjoy the strong coffee Ryan had become so accustomed to. Eating the salty ham and cold biscuits and scarffing it down with the scalding coffee, they soon had the fire doused and were bedded down for the night. Ryan spoke, "You sleep, Dill, I'll watch a while."

"Thanks, boss."

As dawn broke across the east, Ryan became aware that someone new had entered the camp and was sitting silently by, watching them. Raising up, Ryan spoke, "Dill! Get up. We've got company."

"Don't fret, gentlemen. My name is Tomochichi, and I am Yamacraw. Our camp is not far from here. I've been out this morning for game to take back to our tribe. Having watched you from yesterday, I think you are looking for the old Craven lands. You are hoping to find the flat rock?"

"Why, yes." Extending his hand to Tomochichi, Ryan asked if he'd join them in their first meal of the day.

"No. White man's food is not good. We live off fresh foods. But, you come with me, I'll take you to the flat rock."

Ryan and Bennie John pulled in behind the Indian, and after they'd walked a few hundred yards, Ryan stopped and said, "How much further? We don't want to get lost from where we're camping."

Turning, Tomochichi reached and began breaking twigs both left and right of where they were standing. "You break twigs and when we reach the flat rock, you will be able to turn back to where your camp is." Tomochichi nodded and grinned at the stupidity of these white men. Ryan mentally kicked himself for not remembering his Indian ways! Within what Ryan estimated was nearly half a mile, the Indian stopped and pointed. "Here is the flat rock you seek. I shall leave you now and shall hope to meet you again soon." He reached out first this time to shake hands with both men. He turned and disappeared like an apparition into the trees.

"We both need to be horse whipped for our lack of sense!" And they laughed.

Getting the camp cleaned up and riding the horses up to where the flat rock was found brought them to the west edge of the property. From there, they turned south to head back toward the Savannah. All in all, the land was ideal for a good-sized plantation.

• • •

Ryan had long since bade his California lawyer, Simon Dickens, to request a court copy of his birth certificate from London. Grateful was too mild a word for what Ryan felt for the foresight of Captain Confidence Witherspoon in securing Ryan's legitimacy when he'd taken Ryan on as his cabin boy all those years ago. Ryan's own copy of the important document was left behind with his belongings when he'd been kidnapped after the ship had landed in San Francisco Bay. The London certificate had reached him just before he and Millicent had left California. Knowing his upcoming journey might well be fraught with dangers and pitfalls, he left the document in Brannon's bank for safekeeping until he would need it. Now was the time to have it sent to him.

Ryan Alexander Trenton, along with two men of German extraction—Adam Hohenstein and Louis Hohenstein—became naturalized citizens in city court in Savannah that year. All three men were so elated that they celebrated together with friends that evening at the Zeigler House. As the evening wore on more, and more persons joined the party. It was spoken of for weeks afterward. Ryan became well-known throughout Savannah that night and made many contacts while he was at it. Becoming a veritable "son of Savannah" with all its attendant benefits was heady indeed for the orphan offspring of a London whore.

January 10, 1859
Dear Fletcher and Anna,

The five thousand—plus some—acreage has been bought and at present trees are being felled. A saw mill has been set up on a tributary of the Savannah and construction will soon begin. I need you two here as quickly as you can make your way. I'm staying at The Marshall House on Boughton Street right in downtown Savannah.

Included with this letter is the letter from Attorney Prendergast providing you with any amount of money you may need to get here. Take it to Mister Tower and he'll see that you are accommodated forthwith.

I look forward to seeing you soon. Do not tarry.

Your Servant, Ryan A. Trenton

With the great help from his lawyer, Attorney Oliver Wells, the son of the man who had originally conceived the plans for Claudette's French-Greek Mansion was contacted and sent for. Monsieur Durand Moreau sent word back to Ryan through Oliver Wells the regret that he was not able to travel. His health was extremely precarious. However, he did offer to send the actual architectural plans that his father had drawn up on the building of the DuBois House.

Consequently, along with the letters of explanation from Oliver and Durand, came the large package of the plans of the home. Ryan was ecstatic. Now, all he must do was to sniff out the finest builder Savannah had to offer. This happy quest ended with Mister John Scudder.

When the architectural plans were displayed before John, at once he became animated and full of information as to exactly what would be initially needed. Taking no time to draw a breath, Ryan thought out loud, "You are hired! When can you begin?"

Stopping to look directly at the man who'd been so insistent upon their meeting, John said, "I've got a crew master that will be able to finish up my present project, so I can begin this upcoming Monday morning. Where shall we meet in order that I may begin this job?"

"Come to breakfast at the Marshall House at eight on Monday. What would you like? I'll order our repast to be served in the lower area where we'll be undisturbed and can spend as much time as will be needed."

"Great! I prefer their seafood gumbo over ground corn."

Reaching to shake John's hand, Ryan said, "Keep the plans in your possession. I'll see you for breakfast come Monday."

· · ·

His subsequent meetings with John provided Ryan with a plethora of jobs to be accomplished prior to the actual beginning of the house. Thus, this particular morning found him on the highest portion of his vast property watching the industrious processes occurring below.

· · ·

Within a month after the selected property was legally purchased, Ryan began to look for people to work for him. Dill suggested that they attend the Butler Slave Sale to be held the first week of March at the Ten Broeck Race Course. This would be his best opportunity to get prime slaves to do the labor of harvesting the trees and clearing the land.

March second found Ryan and Dill crowded in with hundreds of others interested in buying while the opportunity was presented. Brushing off every suggestion by Dill, Ryan chose a family of five. Talking with the man of the family, Ryan asked if there were anyone else that they would want to bring along with them. "Yessuh, boss. My Auntie. She be old and not much good but she my auntie. She be left by herself iffn you don't want her."

"Good. Go fetch her and I'll buy all of you together. Meet me over yonder at that table you see." Josiah brought his wife, Dorcas, and his three children: Fannie, Eliza, and young Lewis. And bringing up the rear was elderly Aunt Weesie. The group was so grateful to not be torn apart.

• • •

Dill spoke up. "You're sure a fool, Mister Ryan. You ought'a bought several dozen while you could. What in tarnation do you expect to get out'a an old woman, three kids, and the couple?"

"That's something you need not concern yourself with. My plans do not include the use of slaves to accomplish what I desire. Now, let's get these folks onto my property before nightfall. I'll take them there. You buy provisions enough for several days and bring it to the saw mill site. That's where they'll stay until better quarters are made."

• • •

An ad was placed in *The Savannah Republican* to run consecutively until Ryan had hired as many people as required. He was seeking able-bodied men and women to work his plantation from its very inception in the constant business of tending to house and yards and crops to be grown for profit. At the present time cotton was the major export.

Most of the hired were poor sharecroppers, families of men and women who toiled in competition with the big land owners, who gobbled up every advantage with the slaves who were forced to produce. Sharecroppers even had difficulty in finding a bit of land whereby they could eke out a living for themselves to be shared with their overlord. When word spread that this interloper was offering not just housing, but also wages, as well as their own spot of land to work for themselves alone, and to actually be given papers as freedmen and women, many wondered if this were too good to be true, but still found themselves willing to give it a go.

By the time summer was heavy upon Savannah, there were small houses built and ready for occupancy. Ryan began with no less than twenty-four cabins. Several wells had been dug, all bringing forth fresh, cold water. Some distance away from the water sources, a neat line of outhouses was established, and privet hedges would be planted come early fall. Ryan was determined that every comfort and convenience be available to the people who labored at Narcissus Hill.

The subsequent meetings with John provided Ryan with a plethora of jobs to be accomplished prior to the actual beginning of the house. Thus, this particular morning found him on the highest portion of his vast property watching the industrious processes playing out below. He felt he needed some direction as to where the main house ought to be erected, as well as the house for his overseer. Dill was doing a good job for the needs of the moment, but would be hard-pressed to come up to the standard Ryan was expecting for the smooth running of the entire plantation as a whole. Ryan was anxious for his two friends to get here. He did not have long to wait.

. . .

Fletcher and Anna Morgan—now man and wife—arrived in Savannah via coach on an afternoon in mid-September. They were seated, along with Ryan, in the dining room of the Marshall House. Present were also Bennie John Dill and Gifford and Louisa Prendergast. The group had just finished a most delicious, and filling meal, and were all comfortably seated now, with the men smoking cigars and the ladies twirling the wine in their small crystal glasses, murmuring softly with heads together.

"How was the reception for you two upon your arrival back at Anna's home?" asked Ryan.

Suddenly Anna spoke up. "Mama was overjoyed, but Papa was not quite as agreeable as he ought to've been. Fletcher was almost ready to grab me and run off again, until Mama actually stepped up and took Papa to task! She'd never spoken out against Papa before, but I guess it was such a shock to him that he stepped backward and began to nod in agreement with Mama. Finally, he really did calm down and listened to our story and how I alone had made the decision to leave with Fletcher—how he had taken care of me and treated me so well, and then about you, Mister Trenton. We both told him all about you and exactly what you proposed for us."

"Yes," interjected Fletcher, "I explained it all and finally Mister Borden settled down and agreed it was the best for us to get married and take our places with you as our mentor here in Savannah. Why, the Bordens actually spoke of making the trip here to visit us after we've had ample opportunity to become settled."

"That's excellent news. So, you are now husband and wife?"

They laughed and said together, "Indeed, we are!"

"We'll begin our plans in a few days. Y'all take some time to see Savannah and become acquainted with this area. We'll see to your permanent housing before long. Until then, I do hope this place will suffice as your home?"

"Oh, yes. This is a most beautiful hotel and we're quite comfortable."

"Fine. I will expect you…" glancing over at Fletcher, Ryan said, "to spend a good deal of time with me on site to provide any expertise on the actual placing of field crops, and stables, and pastureland. Oh you know… you are the expert in these matters, are you not?"

"It is something I enjoy doing and I hope to prove myself to be of value to you and the needs of your plantation, sir."

The company stood, shook hands all around, and parted ways. Ryan was pleased with everything that had been discussed.

•   •   •

The three men walked up the incline to the highest place that could be reached—that is, until more timber was cut. The saw mill was running constantly, and the fencing for pasture was being strung. Corrals and barns were already under construction. The blacks as well as the white sharecroppers worked well together. No one was privy to the fact that Ryan's slaves had been given papers of release and also were given a salary exactly as the sharecroppers. The money was doled out every Monday evening. Money to every working man and woman. The only extra dole was given to families with children. If anyone had any gripe about anything, Ryan was available every Wednesday morning from seven until ten. Thus far only non-serious matters had been raised and dealt with easily.

"See that clutch of cedars over beyond where the fence line will be?" Pointing, Fletcher said, "I believe that might be an ideal place for the overseer's home. What do you think, Ryan?"

Squinting somewhat in the bright sunshine, Ryan shaded his eyes and felt sure he was observing the area of which Fletcher was speaking. "So you think that would suit for your home?"

With the quickness of a snake strike, Bennie John spoke up. "Overseer's house? Ain't I your Overseer, Mister Trenton?"

"For all intents and purposes, yes, Bennie John, you have been my right hand man. However, your expertise in the actual daily job of running a plantation of this size will prove to be too much for you. I hired Fletcher for this job before I ever got to Savannah. You, Bennie John, will stay on as Fletcher's right hand man. If that is agreeable. If not, then you shall be given severance pay and can leave at your earliest convenience."

Dill turned red and swore. "Damn! Just when wuz you going to break the news to me? You hired me under false pretenses, sir! I fully expected to run this whole operation for you. I ain't heard no complaint from you yet! I'll be honest with you, sir! I don't much take to playin' second fiddle to no newcomer. Especially one as dandified as this man!" He glared over at Fletcher.

"Sorry to hear that, Mister Dill. Come on, gentlemen. Let's head back. As soon as we're at the hotel, I'll send for Mister Prendergast to draw up the severance and you'll be paid for your work up through this coming month. That should be sufficient?"

"Well now, I don't necessarily want to quit you. It's just that I was under the impression that you hired me for the job of overseer. Am I wrong?"

"Yes, Mister Dill, you are wrong. Never did I ever tell you that you are or were to be the overseer of Narcissus Hill. If you recall, I met you the day I met with Attorney Prendergast. In fact you were seated in the outer office with Mistress Drake. I now assume you overheard my conversation with the lawyer, and when I exited his office, you came to me to offer your services to help me find my way around Savannah. You were never hired to do other than what you have done. Agreed?"

"Okay. I guess I was jumping to conclusions, wasn't I? Will you still keep me on as a helper to you and to Mister Fletcher? I promise to make myself worthy of the pay. You've been more than fair in that department, sir, I must say. Much more fair than other folks around here. Yeah, I'd like to stay on."

"Alright with me, if it's alright with Mister Morgan." Turning toward Fletcher, Ryan asked, "What do you say?"

"I say it's fine with me. But I do suppose we need to plan a dwelling for Mister Dill also. He might want to have someone come stay with him at some future time. He'll need a home for himself."

With that little crisis past, the men returned to the spot where they'd been standing, and Ryan said, "Let's see if we can locate the site for Dill's house, shall we?"

• • •

The transformation of the acreage was phenomenal. Anna and Fletcher were now occupying their lovely home. Anna had begun a small food garden as well as planted some flowers and shrubs around the yard. Bennie John had installed a fence for her and had made himself quite useful. It was evident that his mistrust of Fletcher had dissipated the very day Fletcher had suggested they erect a home for him! He could hardly believe his ears when that idea was said.

The Dill cottage was down beyond the stables, at his own suggestion. He loved horses and made himself useful in suggesting which horses to buy and which to steer clear of. Ryan was impressed by his knowledge of the animals. The stables now housed an even dozen horses and four mules. Soon Bennie John would begin looking for milk cows to buy, and there'd need to be chickens, geese, and guineas too. Pigs would also be bought. He had just the right place for the large sty. Mister Ryan had given him a pretty free hand to take care of this facet of the plantation. He was happy, happier than he ever considered he could ever be.

The Mansion of Narcissus Hill was well under way. Ryan was there constantly. In fact, he'd taken to staying in the small house with Bennie John on the days when it was too late to leave for Savannah.

. . .

By early fall in 1859, Ryan was sitting contentedly on the veranda of his Narcissus Hill Mansion. He cast back into his memories. Thirty four years of life. A most full and wondrous life, now a life of leisure. Now a life he could easily become discontent with. Ryan knew he was a man who thrived on action. He must determine his next course and begin. *Let's see. Millie came visiting me last night holding my son in her arms. Beautiful! They were both so beautiful ... That's it! I need to find a wife and begin my family... to fill Narcissus Hill with my family!*

South Carolina had seceded from the Union, and rumors of impending war were on every tongue. He hoped that his new country wouldn't break apart as was foretold. He'd stick with whatever his countrymen decided to do or not to do. But, back to the present objective: a wife. Entering the house he went directly to his library. "Aunt Weesie! Come to the library."

The old woman rustled into his presence. Standing silently in front of his desk, she asked, "What chu need, Sir?"

"Where are all the calling cards we've gotten since the house was finished? I know you must have put 'em somewhere."

"Yes sir. If you'll jes open that draw in front of yore belly, you can fine 'em all. They's right there." Turning to go, she asked, "Anything else?"

"Yes. How about send to the kitchen for a cup of tea and a small cake or piece of fruit. Also, have Lewis lay a fire here. It's getting right chilly in this room."

Stepping over to the window at his back, she began to close the heavy velvet drapes. "If'n we keeps dis here closed, it'll sho keep out lotsa cold air."

"No, leave 'em open. I like the outdoors and the light coming in. I'll close it up come dark."

"Suit y'self. But hit takes a wholotta more wood to chase de chill widis wide open! But you jes' suit y'self... Anything else?"

"No, thank you, Aunt Weesie." A little taken aback at hearing her tittering laughter at his expense, he smiled and opened the drawer. Reaching in to sort through and pull out every card he could locate, he stacked them as though a deck of cards, and began to search each one with diligence.

The first card was from a Mister and Mistress William Casper, III. He flipped it over, and written in a feminine flowery hand the words said: "at home Wednesday August 25, 1859." That one was certainly too late. He quickly turned them all over and discarded all those which were out of date. He was left with three current invitations.

Coming in from the stables a week later, soaked to the skin, Ryan walked right into Eliza's kitchen domain. "What yo gon' and dun, Masser Ryan? Yo's wet frum top to toe. Set down ri'chere and I'll call Josiah." Stepping to the low door to the wine cellar, she yelled, "Josiah! Git up here now and see to de masser!"

Popping through the small opening, he unfolded his tall, thin self from the ladder and stepped out. "Lor, Massa Ryan, whud you do? Fall inna Savannah?"

"No! I was caught in a thunderstorm. Now come, help with these boots. Weesie, have hot water sent right away up to my bathroom." Ryan silently climbed the polished steps of the curved stairs and once again brought into memory the DuBois Mansion. Halfway up, he stopped and turned to glance downward to the scene below. So much nostalgia. So much of Claudette and Katherine was in this home that he'd expressly built for Millie.

There, on the center table, almost hidden from view by the fall arrangement of flowers, he spied the white envelope. Going back down, he retrieved it and continued upward to his rooms. Laying the envelope, unopened, upon the table by the fire, he entered his bathroom and began to disrobe.

.   .   .

Now, wrapped in the long heavy robe with wool slippers upon his feet, he propped himself up before the glowing, snapping fire and reached to pour a splash of brandy. Lighting a long, brown cigarillo, he reached for the envelope. Nothing on it hinted at where it had originated, but it had seen a good deal of wear and tear. Laying it back upon the table, he nestled back into his chair to contemplate the afternoon. With a sad shake of his head he recalled the fiasco of his outing with the young lady Lily Gadsden, with whom he'd been on a picnic when the unexpected storm had struck.

Mistress Lily was one of seven children belonging to a school master. He and his wife were becoming desperate to get the girl married off. She was by all accounts very healthy and built for childbearing. Lily was anything but lily-like. More akin to a sturdy oak, if one had to compare. But Ryan had been willing to investigate her fitness to produce his offspring. He never had the chance. Ryan had just gotten the heavy linen cloth laid beneath some trees whose leaves were sparse enough for the sun to dapple through, warming the ground somewhat. Lily laid out the biscuits and fried chicken when the bolt of lightning struck, splitting a near tree right down the middle. Lily jumped up, screamed, and ran toward Ryan, knocking him down before he could even get up. The basket was crushed, the horse bucked and went tearing away with the trap bouncing merrily along behind. Ryan saw them bound out of sight around the curved lane, heading to God knew where.

With Lily laying screaming on top of him, he finally rolled her over where at least he'd be able to stand. The drops began, big as marbles. The downpour lasted long enough to get the two picnickers totally soaked. Ryan knew before he even glanced skyward what he would see—there, once again, the beautiful Katherine, smiling at him.

They were every bit of two miles from her home, and by the time they arrived, her mother was frantic, having seen the empty rig sweeping past the house and slowing down only when the horse was at the stable gate. Mistress Gadsden was on the front porch wringing her hands when she spied the two dragging up the lane. She ran out to meet them to find what terrible thing had befallen them, and was flabbergasted to find them both sopping wet! She immediately thought they'd fallen into the Savannah.

Once Lily told her mother exactly what had happened, she began crying again. Ryan apologized profusely, admitting they'd left the broken basket and linen behind. He promised to replace both as soon as possible. To which Mistress Gadsden told him absolutely he would not. She was so sorry their outing had been ruined, but she honestly couldn't understand it at all. It had been dry as a bone there, and no one had heard any thunder. Ryan admitted that it had to have been just a localized happenstance, over before it began. He knew he was lying. He knew Katherine was sending another message in the storm.

•   •   •

Now, smiling, Ryan opened the letter.

July 6, 1859
My Dear Master Trenton,

This will come as no surprise to you, I'm sure. You must return to Mobile as quickly as possible and take Katherine as your wife. She swears she will not leave this place as long as I am alive, and I know there's not much time left for me. She knows nothing of this letter, as I don't want her concerned about my immediate death. I will hold on until I see you back in DuBois House. As soon as you arrive, Mary and Tobias will guide your steps to accomplish everything for your benefit. Please, do not fail to heed this.

Lovingly, Claudette DuBois

"I knew it, I knew it!" he spoke out loud, arose from his chair, and stood before the mirror over the wash stand. "I knew you were calling me, Claudette. In fact, I had the eerie feeling that you were with me even as I left DuBois House." He reached for the bell pull and yanked it several times. Within a couple of minutes, Josiah was opening his door. "We must get me packed for an extended trip. I'll be bringing home Mistress Trenton," he beamed.

The unflustered Josiah never so much as blinked an eye as he set to his chores. He left the room and found Dorcas. "Git all the Master's good clothes ready for a long trip. He'll need everything packed neat, now. I'm down getting the trunks and cases cleaned and aired out. We needs to git everything done right. He's bringing his missus home."

Clapping her hands in delight, Dorcas set about doing all necessary to see that Master Ryan's wardrobe was handled with the best of care for the trip. What a joy to work for such a great man.

Seated at his desk, Ryan soon had instructions written out and then sent for Bennie John. Once the man had presented himself, Ryan informed him that he'd be leaving as soon as possible for an extended trip back to Mobile and would be bringing his wife back to Narcissus Hill. Dill was to see to it that all the luggage was on the next coach headed toward that destination.

At dawn two days later, all his house servants, along with Dill and the Morgan couple, were out in front of his home where he mounted the waiting Whistler. "I'll send word as soon as I've arrived in Mobile, and then again as I leave there on the return trip. Please, stay safe. Look out for one another, and, Dill, see that all hands are paid on time. You know I don't like anyone to need money and not have it."

"You can count on me, sir. I'll be on time, every time." He smiled.

"And you, Anna, don't overdo. We are anxious to welcome that baby here in happiness and health!"

"Oh, yes sir! Fletcher will hardly let me lift a finger. I'll take good care of the newest child of Narcissus Hill. You just be safe and hurry back to us."

Chapter XIX

B y the time he entered the outskirts of Mobile, Ryan had run into many young men who were joining the Army of the Confederate States. Already there were a number of Southern states that had seceded from the Union, with more expected to join forces. Alabama had, as yet, not joined them, but Ryan expected it to occur. Presently, he was not interested in the upheaval of the country. He was interested in getting his business attended to and getting DuBois House closed up and transferring Katherine and her entourage to Narcissus Hill.

Ryan felt that ultimately everything would be settled and war would be fought only over cigars and brandy. It was with a light heart that he entered the familiar wide tree-lined lane heading to DuBois House. He knew Claudette would be alive and holding on until he could get there and she could see himself in person. He began to somewhat understand the powers possessed by the little lady and knew she must not be held lightly in esteem.

There it was, the shining jewel of Mobile, shimmering in the near distance. It appeared to move as something alive. As he entered the wide open lawn, his eyes lifted to the glassed-in widow's walk high atop the roof, and he saw a flicker of black silk moving toward the stairway door and out of sight. As his footstep struck the porch, the front door was swung wide by Absalom, who bowed and ushered him in. Ryan was stunned to see the black gauze strung over the chandeliers and mirrors throughout the great hall. Halting where he was, he looked at Absalom and opened his mouth to ask, but Absalom answered his silent question. "Mistress Claudette passed on last evening, sir. Mistress Katherine is in here with her." He motioned with a gesture as they walked down the hall toward the library, where Ryan remembered, *her room is on the left*. Absalom opened the door, and Katherine rose from her chair next to Claudette's high bed. She came silently toward Ryan with hands outstretched. Her face was crumbling with huge tears that flowed unchecked in rivulets down her beautiful cheeks. She wore pale blue silk taffeta that matched her eyes, the ever-present ribbon holding back the masses of dark curls.

Taking her into his arms to let her sob until she lacked the strength to continue, he took these few moments to be thrown off-kilter, realizing it must have been Claudette he'd seen from the widow's walk, making sure he'd arrived at last. He filed this information away for another time of introspection, when he had more time to assimilate the ramifications.

Seating Katherine nearby in a chair, Ryan slipped over to the bed and lifted the black veil from Claudette's face to gaze at this amazing woman. His heart clenched as he drew a ragged breath and leaned over to kiss the cold cheek. At that instant he felt a wind stir in the room and watched as it moved the drapery and swayed the candle flames. Glancing at Katherine he saw she was completely unaware of this occurrence. He felt sure that Claudette was there to bid him welcome and place her blessing upon them. He experienced a small chill of delight in knowing he'd been privy to such an encounter. He replaced the veil and took Katherine's hand as he led her from the room.

•   •   •

Absalom was waiting in the hall, and walked behind them to the sunny east salon. Katherine walked on through and out the doors to stand at the far edge of the stone patio. Absalom pulled the bell. Mary, who'd grown into a most beautiful woman, materialized from nowhere almost instantly, came, and without any fanfare put her arms around Ryan and hugged him. "We're all so glad you are here. Miz Claudette said you'd come today for sure and we never doubted it. In fact, we've already sent word to cousin Clarence. He sent word that he'd be here before sunset this evening for the wedding."

Ryan was cognizant of the fact that he'd just have to get used to this group of people who were more of a family of equals than of servants and masters. He held Mary close and kissed her salty cheek, whispering, "Does Katherine know we're to wed?"

"Yes sir. It was discussed right after you left her all those years ago."

"How did she take to the idea?"

"Oh, she told Grand Maman that she'd felt it the minute she touched your hand when she'd been brought to greet you the night you arrived, but that she knew for sure when you went with her out into the storm."

Ryan nodded silently and went outside to stand with Katherine, and pondered to himself that if he'd known then what he knew now, it would have saved a few suits of clothes and a few nice dresses from ruin. He nodded and smiled knowingly to himself, and Katherine turned toward him and lifted her face for a kiss. He obliged.

• • •

The entire household stood silently in the rotunda at the base of the spiral staircase as Katherine descended, wearing her bridal attire. She was stunning in the pearl-colored silk with pearls around her throat and on her earlobes. Ryan felt the breeze stirring at his back and knew Claudette was back to witness this union. He wondered offhandedly if she would be putting in appearances throughout their marriage. He'd rather her not visit their bridal bedroom, thank you! Gently he chuckled to himself as Father Clarence glanced at his nervous bridegroom.

Father Clarence would be speaking over the body of the Lady Claudette tomorrow morning, but presently no one considered anything amiss having the deceased not twenty yards away, lying on her bed in permanent repose. "Do you have the ring?"

"Yes." Reaching into his waistcoat pocket, Ryan brought forth the simple wide gold band he'd kept near his heart these past years. Now he brought it to his lips with a farewell kiss, and handed it over to the Priest.

"Beloveds. Today we bring together these two here in this company as well as before God Almighty, to be joined..."

Katherine had kept her eyes on Ryan's face the entire time, knowing every plane. She'd memorized them the day she had kissed him in the storm four years back. Even then she knew this day would come, she was not privy to exactly when it would take place. But she never doubted that it would.

As quickly as it had begun, it was completed. All documents were signed, and hugs and kisses, and congratulations were accomplished as Ryan and Katherine became husband and wife. Clarence spoke. "I am so sorry to have to leave before the refreshments and festivities, but I've a sermon to prepare for our Grand Maman's send off. I'll see you all at nine o'clock tomorrow morning at the church."

So, Father Clarence is the priest in the painting. I recall seeing that the first night I arrived here. Being a kinsman, will he possibly have any objections to my taking my bride away from here—all the way to Carolina? I'll concern myself with that later on. For now I shall celebrate this new phase in my life. I need a sip of whiskey. Maybe Absalom will join me.

•　•　•

Attorney Oliver Wells had been at the funeral service three weeks ago and was now seated with Ryan, Katherine, Absalom, Mary, Tobias, and Father Clarence in the library. It seems Claudette had known what Ryan would want and had fairly well tied her wishes with a double knot. The DuBois House would be maintained under the direction of Absalom, Mary, and Tobias with the remainder of the staff living there until their deaths, but would remain the absolute property of Katherine. No one would ever wrest it from her hands. If, for any reason, Katherine should leave DuBois House, then Oliver would see her wishes carried out during her absence.

Father Clarence would continue to receive the allotted monies every month with yearly advancements in that allotment made, as in the past.

The entire lot of DuBois jewels on the property as well as in the bank vault would belong solely to Katherine. It would never be part of a dowry but could be dispensed as Katherine saw fit, only must be disclosed within a legal and binding document under her supervision.

Looking at Ryan, Oliver asked, "Can you abide by these stipulations, sir?"

Silently he nodded.

"Now the final wishes of Madame Claudette. You, Mister Trenton are given total and complete authority over the businesses and holdings here in America as well as in France." Sliding a stack of documents across the desk to Ryan, he continued. "The three attorneys named upon the top sheet are in full compliance and understanding of your role in this portion of the will. Any alterations to be accomplished by you must be dealt with first through these men. Their job is not to sway you one way or the other, but simply to see your every directive is carried out to your satisfaction." Sitting back in the chair, he directed his eyes into Ryan's and said, "Madame Claudette was a very astute woman, so I must trust that she knows you inside and out, or she'd never have put this much power in one individual. I hope you realize how great and vast is this fortune."

Nodding, Ryan said, "I shall not disappoint this family nor the business partners concerned in these holdings. And I can say I am happy to accommodate my new family and abide by the stipulations to the best of my ability." Ryan could swear he felt the brush of a light kiss at the back of his neck as he bent to sign the documents. He just had to turn around to see if he could catch a glimpse of Claudette's presence. But there was nothing, not even a stirring of the gossamer curtains that hung at the window. Those around the desk smiled, except for Oliver, who look somewhat disconcerted at Ryan's inattention for the moment.

•   •   •

Oliver had been invited, but declined. The household held a celebration of sorts, with the cooking of a pig and all the accompanying foods. Many well-wishers arrived to join the gathering and stayed well into the night. Ryan had been overjoyed to see the stately clerk of the Hotel DeVille, as well as Madam Montparssant and young Jimmy Chu. Many of the contacts he'd met and done business with in Mobile were there. What a great occasion to reacquaint himself with this group of folks.

During the festivities, he'd shaken hands and been slapped on the back so many times by the many well-wishers and at such a rate that, in a fit of irony, he hoped Claudette had not been struck through, for he'd noted her presence almost daily at one time or another, to the point he would find himself actually talking to the air around himself when he knew no one was near. The party finally began to dissipate around two o'clock and Ryan felt he could slip away to his chamber without notice. He knew Katherine had left some while ago and would be sound asleep by now.

Chapter XX

T he newly-purchased coach was sturdy-looking enough, Ryan thought, to make the long journey back to Carolina and Narcissus Hill. Trunks had been sent ahead of the company that now was ready to depart. All the family Katherine had in Mobile gathered on the front porch and out in the yard to bid them goodbye. Ryan knew this was difficult for both his wife, as well as young Mary. He silently vowed to himself and to Claudette that he would move heaven and earth to keep them safe from harm and to see always to their happiness. He reached his arm out to wave goodbye and felt the breeze kiss his fingertips.

•   •   •

Journeying across the country, with Whistler trotting behind, Ryan did not push to complete the trip. He did not want to tire man nor beast, and so the return trip to Savannah was more or less an extended honeymoon. They stopped at the most comfortable inns that could be found. The roads were fairly good as long as the weather was dry, and the heavy coach, being deeply slung, afforded the passengers some small degree of comfort.

"How much further is it, Ryan?" she asked, glancing at the passing vistas.

"We should be entering Savannah tomorrow evening. Just one more day, and we'll be home, Katherine. I'm as anxious as you for us to be there. I pray you will feel welcome—as if you were back in DuBois House."

Looking directly at Ryan, she shook her head. "I doubt anyplace can rival DuBois House, Ryan. I've never known another home but there. But we shall see. I do promise to try to transfer my heart to Narcissus Hill. With you there, it shall be easier to accomplish." She smiled. "Tell me something about it."

"Let's see now. It is about as large as DuBois House, and it does have the double porches around, too."

"No widow's walk?"

"Absolutely, there's a widow's walk for your storm enjoyment! There just aren't as many magnolia trees around Narcissus Hill as at DuBois House yet. But you can have whatever you desire planted where you desire. I want you to be happy there. I'll see to it that every whim is answered and met to your satisfaction."

Leaning over to him, she pressed against him and laid her head on his shoulder. "I love you, Ryan. Always have. Always will. I want you to be happy too. I pray we'll have a houseful of children." Sitting back to look once again into his eyes, she said, "You do want children, don't you?"

"More than anything. Yes, I do want children. And, God willing, we'll fill Narcissus Hill with them."

"Yes! God willing."

• • •

For the past week Fannie, Eliza, and Lewis had taken turns in the widow's walk expectantly waiting for the arrival of Mister Ryan and the new missus. At last, Lewis spied the big coach tearing down the shaded lane with Whistler bringing up the rear. Scrambling down the stairs and racing down the hall to the rotunda, screaming at the top of his lungs, the boy cried, "Hurry! Hurry! I see the carriage coming. They's here! Hurry, y'all. They's here."

Footsteps could be heard running from every direction and brought the excited voices of the house crew. Dorcas had cooked special meals now for three days running, just hoping each one would be the one to greet Mister Ryan. Lor' she loved that man. As the family met in the rotunda, Dorcas and Josiah looked the children over to see they were presentable. "Where's Auntie?"

"She be standing right there, Mama," said Eliza, pointing.

"Oh, there Auntie, I clean overlooked you—you so small an'all." They all laughed. "Quick now, let's git to the porch."

With doors swung wide and the group standing like sentinels with grins swiping each shining face, Ryan was struck with a twist in his heart at his huge love for his family here, and for his home.

The coach door was opened, and Ryan helped Katherine down to stand a moment to get her bearings. She looked up at the greeters and saw love radiating from each face. *Why, the little ole lady there reminds me so of Grand Maman, and there is a Mary, and a Toby, and some others too. Let them love me, please, Lord.*

"Katherine, let me introduce you to the house crew. Come, dear." Standing before them, he took each one by the hand and placed it into Katherine's as he gave her their name. "This is Aunt Weesie, Katherine. And this is Dorcas and Josiah—they are husband and wife, and these three are their children. Fannie here's the oldest, then Eliza and young Lewis."

Katherine gently reached to lightly hug Aunt Weesie. "You remind me of my Grand Maman, Aunt Weesie. I hope you'll forgive me if I forget sometimes and call you Grand Maman."

"Chile, you call me whatever you've a mind to. And welcome home, Missus."

•   •   •

After Ryan and Katherine had been helped to their rooms, water was brought for bathing, clothes were shaken and hung, and a lie-down was taken, Katherine roused and rolled over to nestle beside her husband. "It looks just like DuBois House, darling. The only difference really lies in the furnishings and fabrics. Otherwise it's DuBois House over again. How in the world did you do it?"

"I hired the same architect; well, at least he used the same plans done of DuBois House. Even though when I had it built, I did not know you would be my wife, still I wanted this home above all others that I'd seen." He became silent and thoughtful, and continued. "The night BigUn led me on the lane leading to DuBois House, and I was riding toward it, the sight was so inviting in the moonlight and shimmering with drops of rain. The place appeared as though it was magical. It seemed to be bidding me to come into its confines for healing. You see, I was still mourning the loss of Millicent and our child when I got to Mobile. Arriving there did indeed help my soul to heal from that trauma."

"Whatever your reasons were, I'm so glad you did build this home for us. We shall fill it with children. I promise. Now, we'd better dress and get downstairs."

•   •   •

For the next several weeks, Katherine spent her days getting to know every inch of the house and gardens. She seemed to be everywhere. She and Anna became very close and Katherine was enamored with baby Sarah Rebecca. Holding Becky was Katherine's favorite pastime. She could hardly wait for a baby of her own to love and spoil.

The weeks flew into months, the months saw the seasons come and go, and Katherine despaired of having a child. Finally, she became resigned to the fact that there would be no babies. She and Ryan somehow spoke of their lack of children less and less. After a while they simply never brought up the subject at all.

It wasn't until September of 1860 that suddenly Katherine realized she'd not had her menses that month; indeed, she had not received "her visitor" for August either! Immediately she sought out Anna. Knocking on the door of their home and not waiting for an answer, Katherine called out, "Anna! Anna! Are you here?"

Opening the door with Becky half-dressed in her arms and with fright in her eyes, Anna asked, "Kate, are you alright? What's wrong? Is everyone okay?"

Pushing herself into the house and closing the door behind her, Katherine was grinning from ear to ear. "I think I'm going to have us a baby! A baby! I needed to talk with someone about it before I tell Ryan. Can you take time to talk now?"

"Come on in. Let's go to Becky's room. I've got to finish getting her dressed. We've just had her bath and were getting ready to fix dinner after that. But I've always got time for you. So, you think you're pregnant?"

"Yes. I pray so. I've missed 'the visitor' these last two months. Do you suppose that means I am? Or may be?"

"I believe that would be the initial indication, Kate. We do need to wait one more month and then send for Sister Selena. She's the best midwife in Savannah. She'll check you out and if she finds you are pregnant, then she can get Doctor Ballard to begin seeing you. He'll be able to come pretty close to telling you about when to expect the baby to be born."

"Oh, I can hardly wait for October to come and go. I pray I am really pregnant. Should I mention it to Ryan?"

"I wouldn't. Not yet. Wait to see if you are, then you can surprise him and he won't have to wait as long."

"Oh, Anna, I'm so excited. Help me pray that I am and that everything will be wonderful."

"I shall, darling. I shall. Now come, let's get to the kitchen and see if we can get dinner on the table for Fletcher. He'll be home any time now. Would you like to take dinner with us? There's plenty."

"No, thank you, though. I must get home to see to Ryan's dinner. You know they are together and will be coming in about the same time." Leaning over to kiss both Anna and Becky, Katherine said, "Thank you! Thank you so much. You've made me feel much more satisfied."

· · ·

Upon Sister Selena's exam, Katherine's hopes were confirmed and she was put under the watchful eye of Doctor Ballard. Ryan was ecstatic and kept hoping it wasn't all a dream. *Lord, You've taken care of me all these years. You've given me the best life any man could hope for. Please, take care of Katherine and our child. Is this the destiny You designed for me?*

· · ·

Talk of war escalated. By February 1861, seven Southern states had seceded. A Provisional Constitution of the Confederacy had been adopted in Montgomery, Alabama. Jefferson Davis was unanimously elected President of the Confederacy by delegates to the Montgomery convention.

Ryan, Fletcher, and Bennie John kept each other informed as to the daily changes occurring in and around Savannah. More and more men were leaving to join the Army of the Confederacy established March 6, 1861. Ryan had no intention of joining in this madness. Fletcher had a wife and child he was not willing to leave. Besides, neither man owned slaves, and that was at the crux of all the contention. But Bennie John felt strongly about the States' Rights to own slaves and so sought permission from Ryan to join the Army of the Confederacy.

"You have my unwilling agreement to let you go, Bennie John. You have proven to be worth every bit of your pay and then some. Once this conflagration has burned itself out, you find your way back home and you will always have a place here at Narcissus Hill."

He was packed and gone within the week. Ryan and Fletcher began looking to a sharecropper, Mister Sylvan Preston, to groom for Bennie John Dill's replacement. He was married with three daughters, and they did not expect he would want to go anywhere to fight a war. Ryan had the Dill house enlarged with two more rooms in an attempt to accommodate the Preston family.

Becky was now tottering around and so was Katherine. She was tired most of the time, but the spring months gave her great joy. She loved the blossoms everywhere and spent a good deal of time outside in the gardens slipping from one bench to another.

Feeling a slight "pop" as she stood to head back toward the kitchens, she felt a rush of warm liquid pouring down her legs. Grabbing her dress to snug between her legs, she hobbled toward the door. "Dorcas! Dorcas! Come, help me."

"Lor' Child. Here, let me hep you up these steps. Easy now. What's you gone and done?"

"Something popped and there's wet all down my legs. Do you suppose that's the way it's supposed to be?"

"Um hum. That's the way it's suppose to be, alright. Git on in here and we'll get Lewis to go for the doctor and the sister, honey."

"Should we get Ryan now?"

"Naw, let him be for a while. You don't want him here worryin' you to death about it. You'll do better without him until jes' before your baby opens the door to this ole world. Then they'll send for your man, honey. Now, come on."

• • •

Supper was on the table when Ryan came in. "I'm famished, Dorcas. It smells wonderful. I'll be right down as soon as I've washed up a bit."

"Naw, sir. Mister Ryan. You needs to clean up down here this time. Your wife is asleep upstairs and doesn't need to be disturbed. She's had a trying day. You give her a little time to rest. Alright?"

"Well, if you say so. You sure she's okay?"

"Oh yes, sir. I'll fix her a tray in a few minutes."

"Why are you going to fix her a tray if she's resting, Dorcas?"

"I just figured … I kinda wanted … was trying to see…"

"Dorcas! Tell me now what exactly do you mean."

"Awwww. Sister Selena is up with her. The baby is on the way but not ready to put in an appearance. It'll be some time yet, and I didn't want you to worry nor did I want you to bother her."

"For goodness sake, Dorcas. You could have said that before. *The baby!*" Ryan tore out of the room and up the stairs three at a time. Pounding down the hall, he reached the room and grabbed the knob. Locked! Rattling the knob, Ryan lifted his hand to pound on the door, when it was swung inward by Sister Selena, who pushed him back into the hall and shushed him all in the same fluid move.

"Mister Trenton! Get hold of yourself. Your wife does not need your idiocy and brainless interference at this point in time. She is doing very well without your help. She is in heavy labor and if all continues as it should, we shall send for the doctor within the next hour or two. Your staff have their instructions and you can rest assured she is in excellent condition. Your child should make an appearance before the night is much further gone. Now, go and have your supper. Take your rest while you can. You're going to need it later on when your baby wants to stay up all night and you want to sleep." She shoved him toward the stairs.

Who can argue with a nun? He slunk back into the petite dining room where Dorcas had laid his supper and began to eat. Too late he realized he'd not washed his hands and face. After supper he went up to his bathroom and performed his ablutions and redressed in comfortable house clothes and slippers. Retreating down the stairs, he met the doctor as he was let in by Josiah. "Good evening, Mister Trenton. I see you are to be a father in the very near future?"

"With your help, sir, I do hope so. I'm heading in to the library for a smoke and a brandy. If you find time you might want to join me there." *Cannot believe I'm this calm. Did Dorcas put laudanum in my supper?*

With a wide smile, Doctor Ballard said, "I shall. If your wife is going to be somewhat longer, then I certainly shall. But we'll see. Meantime, you just relax and remember the good times, son. I'll see myself up."

•   •   •

Ryan felt himself being shaken. "Wake up. Wake up, Mister Ryan. You's a Daddy. Wake up."

"What? I'm a daddy? Daddy? When?"

"Just now. Doctor Ballard sent word for you to come on up."

Leaping up and taking the stairs with his feet barely hitting the treads, he quickly headed to Katherine's room. The door was already standing ajar, and he pushed himself into the warm chamber. Doctor Ballard was rolling down his sleeves, Sister Selena was folding clothes in a pile, Dorcas was carting out towels and pans, and Katherine was lying, white-faced and silent, with eyes closed and lips slightly open. Her hair was damp and matted. She looked beautiful but wrung out. His eyes filled with tears that quickly ran over and streamed down his cheeks. *God, what had she been through? This thing of giving birth is nothing to be sneezed at. Where is the babe?*

"Where is the baby?"

"Is that all you're interested in?" asked Katherine.

Rushing to the bed, Ryan leaned down and took her into his arms. "No, darling. No. I thought you were asleep."

"I know. I saw you looking over everything. I see your tears of love and compassion. I want you to know that I am fine. Doctor Ballard says I did wonderfully well for a first labor. Only eight hours." Drawing back, she drew back the covers from the far side of the bed and reached for the babe wrapped snuggly in a soft blanket. Handing the baby over to her husband, she said, "Meet your son."

Taking the bundle into his arms, his face crumbled. He sobbed openly, looked toward the ceiling, and spoke, "Lord, at last I know why I was born. Why You've kept me alive. Why You brought Katherine through the storms. Why You have never left me. I thank you Lord for Your faith in me that I can care for and protect these that you've put in my care. Thank you Lord." Turning his tear stained cheeks he laid them against the downy cheek of his precious son.

The birth date of Ryan Alphonse Trenton was April 12, 1861—the day Fort Sumter was fired upon by the Confederacy to take it from Union control.

By mid-summer the Union had begun to blockade Southern ports in an attempt to preclude goods from leaving or entering. These efforts were proving effective in "starving" the South, so in retaliation stalwart sea captains began serious efforts to thwart the blockades. Ryan was instrumental in manning a ship he named the *Katie Girl*. She became notorious for slipping through the blockades time after time. The supplies were shipped to foreign ports and brought in to Southern ports. Ryan found himself in Mobile Bay on more than one occasion and was able to stay at DuBois House. But success was short-lived. Before long, by sheer outnumbering, the Confederacy began to buckle.

The war devastated the South. She fought a valiant battle for the desire to hold and keep slavery intact, but it was not to be. She was driven to her knees by the superiority of the Union forces—which had the advantage of hard industry to supply her lines.

The winter of 1864 rang the death knell for the Confederacy. Union General Sherman swept his troops down into Georgia, destroying crops, homes, bridges, railways, cattle, and anything else to kill any incentive to retaliate. Atlanta was burned and those not killed were scattered like debris in a hurricane. He raped the land into complete submission as his forces headed toward Savannah. Ryan had been back in Narcissus Hill only a week when word came that Sherman's arrival was imminent. Having enough sense to realize the war was over for the South, he gathered with a delegation of aldermen—including another wealthy and prominent businessman, Solomon Zeigler, and some influential ladies, along with Mayor Richard Dennis Arnold. Word was then sent requesting a meeting with General Sherman. Their proposition stipulated that there would be no resistance, and for the surrender of Savannah they wanted the assurance that General Geary would protect the city's citizens and all their property. Geary telegraphed Sherman, who advised him to accept that offer. Mayor Arnold formally presented Geary with the key to the city, and Sherman's men, led by Geary's division formally occupied Savannah that same day. This decision saved Savannah from annihilation on December 21, 1864.

. . .

Suffering throughout the Southern states was horrific. Starvation became a burden heavy upon the backs of all. Roving bands of freed slaves who had no direction or help often murdered out of sheer desperation. Ryan and the white sharecroppers that worked his plantation were constantly being set upon by desperate blacks and displaced whites. As much as was possible, food was shared and clothing given. The plantation houses became full of lost people who moved in to seek shelter and sustenance. Ryan and Fletcher put everyone to work building more dwellings and clearing more land. The winter months were more difficult, but it seemed as though the ones who came and stayed decided to use their opportunity to add to the expansion, knowing it would ultimately benefit them all.

Making it through the cooler winter months gave them the strength to face the spring with hope and renewed energy. The plantation flourished and became a model of efficiency and cooperation between workers and bosses. Neither desired to take advantage over the other.

By mid-July, 1865, the heat was stifling and the sky portended rain. The people as well as the land were needing some relief. Ryan was seated, with Fletcher and Sylvan Preston, in the shade of the moss-hung oak which stood in the middle of Katherine's water garden. She had dug a small fish pond from an underground spring which had been located during the excavation for shrub planting. The little pond contained several large goldfish which had made it through the winter, with the addition of plants in which they could hide.

"Looks like we might just get a little shower," said Fletcher.

"Yep, I sure hope so. We need it bad," agreed Sylvan.

"We can find out," said Ryan.

"How?" both asked together.

"Katherine will know. I'll be right back."

Leaving the men still seated on the bench, Ryan went into the house, through the kitchen, and up to the nursery where he knew he'd find his wife with the children.

Opening the door, he found all four asleep on the cot. What a beautiful picture. Katherine with her dress open to expose one plump breast to the suckling lips of six-month-old baby Abby. Toward the foot of the bed were four-year-old Al with his arms around his two-year-old brother Emile. Sitting in silent security and nodding as she hummed some unknown song was Auntie Weesie.

Backing out of the door, he closed it quietly. *This my life. My blessed life. Thank You, Lord.*

"Yet one more, Ryan."

"Who?" Turning quickly to see exactly where those words had come from, Ryan saw there was no one evident. Knowing full well he did hear a voice, he was shaken a bit, but having dealt in the past with visits by Claudette, this new phenomenon created no fear, only questions. *What does 'yet one more' mean?* Deliberately dropping this from his mind, he descended the stairs and, going through the kitchen, he stopped to lift three apples from the shallow tray and exited the door. Seating himself once more by his companions, he handed them an apple each, and explained, "Kate was asleep, and I didn't have the heart to awaken her. But we can enjoy these apples and contemplate the rain."

•　•　•

The following afternoon, Ryan was studying plans for an expansion of acreage to dedicate to another field of corn production, when Josiah entered with a letter that had come earlier that day. Laying it near his arm, Josiah said, "Here's yo mail, sir."

"Thank you, Josiah. Will you see to filling the brandy decanter, please?"

"Right away, sir." Taking the empty decanter, Josiah left the library. Slitting open the large envelope, Ryan opened the folded paper.

July 3, 1865
Greetings to You and Yours,

This day finds me bearing both good news and bad news. As your good friend, and knowing your penchant for dealing with the worst first, then into the best last, let me break the news that our beautiful Pakuma was killed last week by a drunken miner staying at Coloma Hotel. He caught her in the upstairs hall and dragged her into his chamber where he accosted her and choked her to death. He fled off to God knows where, but with Claymore's son, Randall, on his tail, he's sure to be found and brought to face judgment.

Pakuma's death has rattled this settlement. She had become such a rich part of our town. We all were amazed by her strength and common-sense approach to taking care of Lokni.

This is where the good news comes in. Pakuma had a son about nine months after you and Millicent left us. There's no denying you are the father of this boy. He is your image, except that his hair is black. In all other respects he's you made over. Anyway, to get to the point, Wauna wants him sent to you. Sewatee is too old to keep him. Besides, Lokni has been raised as white and knows nothing but 'our ways.' Pakuma has seen to it that he's received as much education as is available to us here. The boy is very intelligent—like yourself, and he knows his father is white, he just doesn't know you. YET!

You need to either come get him yourself, or give me permission and I will see him on the next stage headed to Savannah.

Meantime, he is well cared for. Living in the small house built by Pakuma for herself, Wauna, and the sisters. He has done very well (having only women to live with). Presently he works for Paul Robertson's family, doing whatever, wherever he's needed.

Ryan, you have a very handsome lad. His full name—given by Pakuma—is Alexander Lokni Trenton. You can be proud.

Let me hear from you by return mail.

Sincerely, Simon Dickens, Atty. at Law

So! This is what was meant by the voice that told me there was 'yet one more'!

Sitting awestruck, Ryan's thought processes were scattering with a wondrous amount of questions. All of which had no answers. The greatest of which was why Pakuma never sent word of the birth of his son. Through a quick cyphering, Ryan determined that the boy would be about twelve years old. Yes, his son must come to Savannah as soon as it could be arranged. *I'll send a telegram out to Simon tomorrow... after I talk with Katherine. I wonder what she'll think. We'll soon find out. Okay, Lord, I'm ready now for my destiny to be fulfilled, at least up to this point. No more surprises, please. This son of mine deserves all the good I can supply... especially since his mother is gone. Protect him and bring him to me as quickly as possible. Katherine will understand. Katherine will understand.*

Standing in the rotunda, Ryan looked up to see Katherine coming down the circular stair, her eyes on his face. She stopped on the lowest step and said, "Send for him, Ryan. He too is our son."

"How did you know about Lokni?"

"Now Ryan, you know Grand Maman keeps me up on everything. Don't be so surprised. You know she'll never leave us." Stepping down to face her husband, she lifted her arms to encircle his comforting body, and laid her head against his beating heart. Looking upward, she smiled and kissed his lips. "She really doesn't mean any harm. She stays because she knows we love her and she loves still being part of our lives and the lives of our children."

"I guess I ought not be surprised. I'm forever running into her spirit. At least, I think it has to be her, because she feels like air kisses."

"That's Grand Maman, alright. By the way, even though I'm still nursing Abby, she told me this morning that I'm pregnant again."

Stepping backward and holding his wife at arms' length, he grinned unashamedly. "God is ever full of surprises. He continues to enlarge my destiny, but is there any way you can keep her out of our bed chamber?"

"Really, darling, I'm not a miracle worker."

Finis

Made in the USA
Middletown, DE
19 January 2022